THOMAS TREW
AND THE HIDDEN PEOPLE

THOMAS TREW
AND THE HIDDEN PEOPLE
THE

SOPHIE MASSON

Illustrated by Ted Dewan

Hodder
Children's
Books

A division of Hachette Children's Books

A Catalogue record for this book is available from
the British Library

ISBN-10: 0 340 89484 9
ISBN-13: 978 0 340 89484 2

Typeset in Weiss by Avon DataSet Ltd,
Bidford on Avon, Warwickshire

The paper and board used in this paperback by Hodder Children's
Books are natural recyclable products made from wood grown in
sustainable forests. The manufacturing processes conform to the
environmental regulations of the country of origin.

Hodder Children's Books
a division of Hachette Children's Books
338 Euston Road
London NW1 3BH

To Beverley, with many thanks

ONE

'There's a dwarf in the hall,' said Thomas Trew to his father, one grey London afternoon.

His father Gareth didn't even look up from his desk. Ever since he'd lost his job, he was always doing sums, trying to make two and two equal twenty-two, not four.

'There's a dwarf in the hall, Dad,' Thomas repeated. 'And he's with a lady who's dressed like a rainbow.'

'Mmm,' murmured Gareth, vaguely. He was used to Thomas's stories about people only he could see. Everyone thought Thomas was a bit weird, even his dad. The only person who hadn't was Thomas's mother, Mab; but she was dead.

1

Thomas didn't mind what people thought. That was their problem, not his. Ever since he could remember, he'd seen people who weren't there, and heard things that no one else heard. And he *knew* they were real.

'Dad! They say I've got to go to Owlchurch. They say you promised Mum!'

His father jumped up, scattering scribbled papers everywhere. 'They do, do they?' He rushed to the hall. And there he saw that Thomas wasn't making it up.

The dwarf had black whiskers and black eyes, and wore a very old suit, much too big for him. The lady was a bit taller. She had wild grey hair and narrow green eyes. She wore a rainbow mix of colours: red, orange, yellow, green, blue, purple.

'I'm Angelica Eyebright of the Hidden People, Middler Country, Owlchurch branch,' she said, briskly, before Gareth could say a word. 'And this is Adverse Camber, also of the Hidden People, etcetera.'

Thomas beamed. 'I've seen people like you, lots of times, out of the corner of my eye. I wondered when you'd talk to me.'

'Sorry to dodge about like that,' smiled Angelica Eyebright. 'Had to, you know. Couldn't speak to you till you were ready.'

Gareth found his voice. 'Wait on! You're not supposed to contact him till he's ten! That's not till August!'

Angelica Eyebright looked shifty. 'Things have changed. He has to come *now*.'

Gareth folded his arms. 'What's the big hurry?'

Thomas stared at his father. 'Dad! Do you know these people?'

It was Gareth's turn to look shifty. 'Not exactly . . . but your mother . . . she did say that . . . well—'

Angelica Eyebright interrupted. 'You still haven't told him, Gareth Trew! Well, *really!*' She turned to Thomas. Her eyes flashed. 'He was supposed to tell you. Ages ago. You are a

Rymer, Thomas. A Rymer, like your dear mother Mab was before you. And it's time you came and lived with us.'

Thomas's heart beat fast. 'A Rymer? What's a Rymer?'

Then Adverse Camber spoke for the first time. His voice was very deep, like the rumble of distant thunder. 'A Rymer sees and hears things other people can't. A Rymer can travel easily between the worlds.'

'Between the worlds?' breathed Thomas. 'What worlds?'

'Our world – the Hidden World; and the world of humans, which we call the Obvious World,' said the dwarf, gravely.

'The Hidden World is the source of dreams and magic,' added Angelica. 'There are two kinds of humans who can go there. Magicians – witches, wizards, enchanters and so on. And Rymers. With a few trusted exceptions, magicians can only come for short, supervised visits. We hold conventions and conferences

5

and workshops for them. But they're not allowed just to come and go as they please.'

'Have to keep an eye on magicians. They're ambitious. Out for what they can get. They snoop. They often try to trick us and pinch magic,' said Adverse.

Angelica said, 'Magicians are our customers. But Rymers – they're our *friends*. They come into our world not to learn about magic, but to learn about *us*. You see, they're our ambassadors back to the Obvious World, the strongest link between the two worlds. So they can live with us for as long as they want.'

'When they leave us,' said Adverse, 'we give them a precious gift to take back to the Obvious World. A gift they can use for the rest of their lives. The gift of poetry. Of story. Of art. Of prophecy. Of music . . .'

Thomas only half remembered his mother. She'd died when he was four years old. But he did remember one thing very clearly. She'd played the flute, beautifully. He heard it sometimes, in his dreams. Music was what she'd brought back from the Hidden World, he thought.

'We've been friends with the Rymers for a long time,' went on Angelica. 'You see, centuries ago, a Rymer helped us when we were in great danger. We've never forgotten. After that, we vowed eternal friendship with all Rymers.'

'And I'm one of them?'

'You are indeed. So was your mother. So was her uncle. Not everyone in your mother's family has been a Rymer, though; it skips whole generations sometimes. And there are Rymers to be found all over the world. But you have one thing in common. You're all descended from that first Rymer, centuries ago.' She smiled. 'He even had the same first name as you – Thomas the Rymer. We called him True Tom.'

'Now just hang on a minute,' said Gareth, finally getting a word in. 'This is all very well, but you still haven't explained what the big hurry is. We have a right to know!'

Adverse and Angelica shot a glance at each other. 'Thing is,' said Angelica, slowly, 'we think the Uncouthers may be on the move again.'

'Uncouthers?' Thomas repeated, uneasily.

'You see, Thomas, there are different peoples living in the Hidden World,' said Adverse Camber. 'The Middlers – that's us. We live on the lowlands. The Ariels – they come from the sky-country. The Seafolk – they live in the oceans and seas. The Montaynards – they live in the rocks and the mountains. And then there's the Uncouthers. They live deep underground, in the dark city of Pandemonium. They make nightmares, and sell evil magic to sorcerers, and they don't get on with the rest of us.'

Angelica said, 'That's what the Rymer helped us with, long ago. Back then the Uncouthers declared war on the rest of the Hidden People, and tried to take over our world. True Tom could have simply gone back to the Obvious World. But he didn't. He helped us fight.'

'We defeated the Uncouthers,' added the dwarf. 'Since then, they've been bound by a strict peace treaty. They've tried to get around it once or twice. In the last century or so, it's been OK, because their Queen isn't interested in war. But we've heard she is about to give up her throne to her son. And we think he's got big plans to try and take over the worlds again.'

'What will happen if he does?'

'He'll stop good dreams,' said Adverse, quietly. 'Nightmares will flood the Obvious World. Everyone will be scared to go to sleep. People will go mad. Governments will fall. Even magicians and Rymers will be helpless. The world will go dark. The Uncouthers will rule everything.'

Thomas shivered.

'Now hang on,' cried Gareth, before Thomas could speak. 'Are you expecting him to fight the Uncouthers? Are you crazy? He might be a Rymer, but he's also my son and I don't want him put in danger.'

'Do you think *we* do?' snapped Angelica Eyebright. 'Of course we don't want him to fight the Uncouthers. He's not ready for that, not yet. But we think he's more at risk if he stays here. We've heard that the Uncouthers are looking for him. They don't know who he is, not yet. But they've always hated the Rymers, since that first one. They've always felt that his part in the war turned the tide against them. If we leave it much longer, they might actually find Thomas. And then . . . well, let's say they'll try their hardest to stop him coming.'

The dwarf said, quietly, 'It's hard for us to protect him here. The effect of nightmares is much stronger here than in our world. Believe me, Mr Trew, Thomas will be much safer in Owlchurch. The Uncouthers won't dare to harm him there. They'll know they have us to reckon with.'

'I still don't know if—' began Gareth, but Thomas interrupted him.

'Dad, I want to go. I *really* want to go. I really *have* to go!'

'Oh, for goodness' sake, Thomas! You can't go on your own . . . you just can't. I would be worried to death.' He rounded on Angelica and the dwarf. 'You're crazy, putting such ideas in his head! He's still young! He needs his father!'

'Of course he does,' said Angelica, calmly. 'That's why you're coming too, Gareth Trew.'

Gareth spluttered. 'Me?'

'The very same. I have a job for you. Managing my business, the Apple Tree Café. You need a job, don't you?'

'Yes, but . . .'

'And don't worry about the house. We'll send a squad of house-pixies to keep it in tiptop shape till you come back. Now then, go and pack, both of you. We need to leave as soon as possible. And don't bother taking too much. There's all you need in Owlchurch.'

Gareth started protesting again. But Thomas took no notice. He raced up the stairs to pack his bag, more excited than he'd ever been in his life. And if he was a little scared too, well, he could cope with that for the moment. Things were really happening, at long last!

TWO

They were soon packed and ready to go. Outside, there was a car waiting for them. It was small and round and jolly, with big headlamps like a pair of eyes, and looked rather too small to fit them all in. But as soon as Adverse Camber opened the driver's door, a grating voice complained, 'Have to let out my girth again, what.' All at once, the car walls puffed out like an inflating balloon.

Adverse saw Thomas's expression. 'Say hello to Metallicus. He gets cross if you don't.'

Gareth looked a bit sick at all this, but Thomas was thrilled. He touched the wall of the car and whispered, 'Hello, Metallicus.

I never knew cars could talk!'

'Ha! Most can't,' grated Metallicus. 'I'm one of a kind. Special, that's me. Now, are you lot getting in, or am I to stand about here all day?'

Adverse Camber winked at Thomas. 'No, we're ready to go, Metallicus,' he said in a humble tone of voice, and jumped into the driver's seat. 'Head for home!'

They headed out to the motorway. Night was falling. They'd been driving for some time when suddenly, Adverse Camber turned sharply left. The car shuddered, bumped and rattled down a narrow little slipway. For an instant, it seemed as if the car wouldn't stay on the road. Thomas screwed his eyes shut. When he opened them a second later, bright sunlight was coming in at the windows!

Angelica Eyebright smiled at his astonishment. 'Our worlds are not in the same time zone, Thomas. Look behind you.'

Thomas did. He could only just see the

motorway very faintly now in the distance, in a fast-vanishing square of black. It was night back there. Long, winter night. But here, it was a beautiful summer's morning!

They drove on for a little while. All around was green countryside – fields, and woods, and sparkling streams. Once or twice, they saw little houses in the distance, with thatched roofs and smoking chimneys. Then, round a bend in the road, Adverse Camber stopped the car. 'Owlchurch!' he proclaimed.

He was pointing at a square, brownstone church tower on the horizon. It was set at each corner with a carved tuft of stone that looked for all the world like an owl's ear. And then Thomas caught sight of something else in the distance. It was a tall, silver church spire, glittering in the blue air. 'What's that?' he said, pointing.

Adverse Camber's mouth turned down. 'Aspire,' he grunted.

Thomas thought he'd said, 'A spire.'

'I know it's a spire,' Thomas said, 'but what is it?'

The dwarf frowned, ferociously. 'It's another Middler village, called Aspire, across the River Riddle from Owlchurch.' Crossly, he engaged the gears. Metallicus grated, 'Watch what you're doing, you clumsy oaf!'

'Oh, shut up,' snapped the dwarf, driving on, rather jerkily. 'Never happy, that's you. Think you'd be better off in Aspire, maybe!'

'Adverse! That'll do!' said Angelica, sharply. She turned to Thomas and his father. 'Aspire and Owlchurch may be neighbours, but we don't see eye to eye. The Aspirants think we're old-fashioned stick-in-the muds.'

'And we think they're trendy snobs,' growled Adverse. 'Jumped-up, stuck-up, butter-wouldn't-melt, phony—'

Angelica cut in, sharply. 'OK, thanks, Adverse, that'll do. Ah, everyone – here we are!'

* * *

Owlchurch nestled in a fold of rounded green hills. Misty woods bordered it on three sides. On the fourth side was a broad silver stream: the River Riddle. The village was not very big, with a few streets leading away from a large village green. There stood the brownstone church they'd seen from the road. This was the church of Saint Tylluan. The saint was pictured in a stained-glass window. He looked rather like a large, spectacled owl.

Around the green were clusters of odd little shops. Some looked as though they'd been built from random scraps of metal and wood. Others were like fanciful cakes: all twists, turrets, curls and iced tiers, in bright colours.

The names were as extraordinary as the shapes: Cumulus Zephyrus's Heavenly Bakery; Morph Onery's Dreaming Emporium; Calliope Nightingale, Musical Instruments; Brigsein Nectar, Grocer; Willy Wisp, Lighting; Monotype Eberhardt, Bookseller;

Hinkypunk Hobthrust's Tricks For All Times; and, finally: Apple Tree Café, Prop., Angelica Eyebright.

The Apple Tree Café certainly didn't look like any café Thomas had ever seen before. In fact, it seemed to be an enormous apple tree that looked half real and half not, like a cartoon. Its trunk was gnarled and pitted and its crown stretched high above them.

The car stopped. Angelica Eyebright jumped out. She walked rapidly to the tree, put a hand on it, and said, 'We're back.' At once, the tree dissolved, like a scene in a film or a video game. And there stood a three-storey house that looked as if it had been built by a mad carpenter, with crazy angles all over the place.

Angelica Eyebright ushered them up the steps. It smelled good inside, a mixture of fresh-cut wood and fresh-baked bread. There were a couple of rooms downstairs, including a big one for the café. Gareth went in there to

take a look. But Thomas followed Angelica Eyebright up the stairs to the second floor, to his new bedroom.

It was the sort of room Thomas had always dreamed of. Not too big, and not too small, but cosy and sunny, with a big round window on to the street. A large soft rug covered much of the floor and there were crowded bookshelves lining two of the walls. The bed was a curtained four-poster, and there was also a low, padded window seat.

'Do you like it?' asked Angelica.

Thomas nodded, eyes shining.

'It was your mother's room, too,' went on Angelica, gently. 'I think she would be very happy to know you are here at last. As happy as we are. Now then, Thomas, I'll leave you to it. I'll be downstairs if you need me.' She went out, shutting the door.

Left alone, Thomas bounced on the bed, to try it out. At once, a soft voice spoke to him from the bed-curtains. 'Welcome to your bed,

Thomas. Tell me where you want to sail off to in your dreams!'

'Wow!' said Thomas, jumping off the bed. He went over to the shelves and pulled out a book. It opened on a picture of a sleeping dragon. Suddenly, the dragon opened one eye, gave a great snort, and opened its mouth. 'Wow!' said Thomas, again, quickly snapping the book shut. He went over to the window seat and knelt on it to look out. As he did so, a sweet voice whispered, 'What tune would you like to hear, Thomas?'

'I really don't know,' said Thomas, taken aback. 'I think that I—'

He jumped. A pebble clattered against the glass. And another. And another. Thomas stared down into the street. There were two children down there, staring up at him. They looked like twins, a boy and a girl, with greenish skin and yellow hair. Catching his eye, they grinned and waved. Thomas waved back. They beckoned. 'Come on outside,' mouthed the boy.

Thomas didn't need to be asked twice. He'd been a bit worried he might be the only child here. He ran down the stairs and out into the street. Then he stopped. Suddenly, he felt rather shy.

'Er . . . hello,' he mumbled.

'Hello,' chorused the children, smiling. Close up, they didn't look exactly human. Their eyes were a strange mixture of yellow and orange, they had sharp pointed faces and ears, and there *seemed* to be little twigs tangled into their wild yellow hair. But they were very friendly.

'You must be True Tom,' said the boy. 'I'm Pinch Gull. This is my twin sister, Patch. We live up there with our mother. She's a herbalist,' he added, pointing up in the direction of the woods.

'Oh, hi, Pinch and Patch,' said Thomas shyly. 'By the way, my name's not really True Tom, but Thomas Trew. I'd prefer to be called Thomas. If you don't mind,' he added, politely.

Pinch laughed. 'No, we don't mind. You can call yourself whatever you like.'

All this while, Patch had not spoken. Now she said, 'But can you *be* what you like?' She spun around, clapped her heels together, and vanished. In her place was a little green frog. It hopped on to Thomas's arm, flopping down with a squidgy feel. He yelled.

'Don't be silly,' scolded the frog in Patch's voice, and jumped off. As soon as it hit the ground, it turned into Patch again.

'My sister likes to show off,' said Pinch, grinning. 'You'll get to know that.' He looked slyly at Thomas, shook his head of yellow hair – and instantly, there was a leopard. A leopard's head mounted on a skinny child's body. Thomas couldn't help laughing.

'What's so funny?' came Pinch's voice out of the snarling mouth. In an instant, he was back to his usual self. He looked sulky now. 'Can *you* do anything like that?'

'No. I wish I could. But I'm just ordinary.'

'No you're not,' said Pinch. '*I'm* ordinary. *You're* different. You're a Rymer. What's more, you're an Obbo.'

'An Obbo?'

'You know – from the *Obvious* World. We've never seen an Obbo before. Except for magicians, and they're dull. All they think about are spells.' He looked wistful. 'What's it like out there, in your world?'

'Boring! Things stay the shape they always are, cars don't talk, beds don't take you sailing, pictures don't come alive, people don't turn into frogs and leopards!'

'It doesn't sound *real*,' said Patch, frowning. 'You're making it up.'

'I am not!' He waved a hand at the shops. 'Like, there's no such thing as a Dreaming Emporium in our world. I don't even know what it is!'

Patch looked amazed. 'Really?' She turned to Pinch. 'Hey, how about we show Thomas?'

'Good idea. Let's go to the bakery first, though,' said Pinch, promptly. 'I'm starving. Aren't you?'

Thomas nodded. He suddenly felt very hungry. No wonder. He hadn't eaten anything since lunch. And that felt like ages and ages ago.

THREE

Cumulus Zephyrus's Heavenly Bakery was very grand. It had white pillars, a golden dome for a roof, and a huge display window. Behind the glass there was an enormous meringue and toffee and chocolate castle with twin, twisted towers. Around this a whole host of little iced cakes was piled, as well as trays of golden pies and savoury rolls. Thomas's mouth watered. Eagerly, he followed the twins into the shop.

The baker was gigantic. Golden-skinned and black-haired, he had large black eyes, with golden pupils. Enormous grey-white wings sprouted from between his shoulder blades. He wore a long black sleeveless tunic, and heavy bronze bangles on his brawny bare arms.

'Mr Zephyrus,' said Pinch, very importantly, 'this is our friend, Thomas. He's a Rymer. He's come to live here!'

Cumulus Zephyrus smiled. 'Welcome, indeed, Thomas! We hope you'll be very happy in Owlchurch.'

'Thank you, sir,' said Thomas, a little overawed. 'I'm sure I will.'

'Thomas really, *really* wants to try one of your cakes, Mr Zephyrus,' said Pinch, hopefully.

The baker laughed. 'And I suppose you'd like to keep him company, eh, you rascals? Choose whatever you like, then.'

Patch's eyes were round. 'Anything?'

'*Anything!* It's a special day, when a Rymer comes to stay with us. Especially one who has the same name as that first one of blessed memory!'

In the end, Thomas chose a chocolate cake,

Pinch a sausage roll and Patch a cream bun. They went outside to eat them.

It was the best chocolate cake Thomas had ever eaten, rich, dark and delicious, but also light and melting as a cloud.

'Good, eh?' Pinch grinned.

'Best baker in all the Hidden World.' Patch nibbled delicately at her bun, like a squirrel. 'He's an Ariel, you know, and they're famous as bakers. But Mr Zephyrus is better than all the others put together. He's won lots of prizes.'

'The Aspirants are always trying to poach him off us,' said Pinch, gulping down the last of his roll.

'They always want the best of everything,' added Patch. 'But they won't get Mr Zephyrus. He really likes it in Owlchurch.'

'Lucky for us!' Pinch licked his fingers. 'OK, let's go to Morph's, then.'

Morph Onery's Dreaming Emporium was a large, noisy workshop. In one corner, people worked at spinning wheels. They had long, grey, skinny arms, like spiders. Thread as fine as gossamer flew through their bony fingers, and shimmered on the wheels. Patch pointed at one spinner. 'See that yarn she's making? That's a flying dream.'

Thomas stared at the fine, light thread. Suddenly he felt an odd tingle in his toes and heels. Then with a rush that knocked him off balance, his feet left the ground.

Patch grabbed at his arm. She pulled him down and marched him firmly away. 'You've got to be careful,' she scolded. 'You could have crashed!'

Pinch beckoned. 'Come and look, Thomas!'

It was a line of weavers at their looms. Each of them was using different coloured strands of spun thread to create amazing cloth that moved and rippled. One of the cloths was like a river: silvery on the surface, with deep greens, blues, and blacks underneath. He was sure he could see fish swimming in the depths.

'Careful!' Pinch shouted, as the river cloth suddenly shifted, rising like a wave towards Thomas. He jumped back.

'Told you to be careful!' Patch hurried him away. 'It's a betweener: one of those half-waking dreams. Can give you a real headache!'

'Never mind,' said Pinch excitedly. 'Come and look at this! This is one of my favourites!'

They had come to what looked like an aquarium, which took up half a wall. But instead of fish, tiny bright insects with long, thin noses flew around what looked like dandelion and thistle flowers. They weren't the colours of dandelions and thistles in the human world, but multicoloured and shimmering, with tiny parachutes on each flower that glittered like pure gold.

As Thomas watched, the insects landed on the flowers. They dipped their noses in, as if they were drinking nectar. But when they lifted their heads up again, Thomas saw that lots of glittering little parachutes were stuck to them. They took off again in a whir of wings, rising up into the air, then vanishing as suddenly as if someone had grabbed them.

'They're so beautiful!' cried Thomas. 'What are they? What are they doing?'

'They're Dream Blowers,' said Pinch. 'One of Morph's most famous ideas. He breeds them, you know.'

'And the flowers are just light, pleasant little dreams,' said Patch. 'The Dream Blowers slip into the Obvious World and just puff all those little parachutes into the air. They land on whoever's closest.'

They moved on, to a section crowded with shelves, each with a series of small cages. In each cage was a little creature. Fascinated, Thomas looked closer. There were tiny birds, minuscule lions, bonsai dogs. And also miniature dragons, griffins, and unicorns. Thomas was fascinated.

'Don't get too close! They bite!' warned Patch.

Pinch laughed. 'You're a chicken, Patch!' He flung open one of the cages. Out flew a screaming little streak of burning brown and gold, straight at Thomas. He fell, dizzily, the creature's tiny hot claws sizzling on his skin, a smell of warm raisins and brandy wafting to his nose.

Shouting, Pinch and Patch threw themselves on the little creature, trying to wrestle it away from Thomas. But it hung on, screaming.

'What's going on here? Why have you let the flapdragon out?' The bellow made Pinch and Patch jump up immediately. A huge hand landed on Thomas's shoulder, and another gently picked up the little creature between finger and thumb.

At once, Thomas's head cleared. He looked up, and saw, not a giant, as he'd expected, but a small, bent old man, black skinned and with sparse white hair, and bare, muscled, blue-tattooed arms. His clothes were shabby, and tangled masses of silver chains hung

over his big chest. But it was his eyes that Thomas noticed especially. They were different colours – a beautiful clear blue and an intense amber-brown – and each eye had a different expression. The brown eye had a soft, forgiving air; the blue a rather fierce one.

Pinch gabbled, 'We can explain, Mr Onery. We were just showing Thomas – you know, he's our new Rymer, Mr Onery – we were showing him the dream-creatures; he . . . he leaned too close, and the flapdragon . . . er . . . escaped.'

'It did, did it?' said Morph Onery, dangerously. Carefully, he put the flapdragon back into its cage and closed the door. It hung there limply on its perch, steaming a little. The Dream-maker turned to Thomas. 'Is that true?'

Thomas shot a glance at the twins. He found Morph scary, but he'd never been a tattletale. 'Yes,' he gulped.

'Hmmph,' said Morph, very suspiciously

indeed. He shrugged. 'Lucky you had your mouth closed,' he observed. 'The flapdragon usually makes a dive for your throat.'

Thomas gulped. 'What . . . what would have happened if he . . .'

'Oh, you'd just have wild, mad dreams for a week or so. A bit tiring and sweaty, but mostly harmless. Well, well. Our new Rymer, eh? Pleased to meet you, Thomas. I knew your mother well. She was lovely. It's great to have her son here.'

Solemnly, he shook hands with Thomas. 'But now I'm afraid I'm going to have to ask you all to go. None of these creatures will be fit to send out tonight, and as to my poor flapdragon, I'm going to have to soothe him for a week.' He shot a sharp glance at the Gull twins. 'Don't let me catch you in here again for a while, Pinch and Patch Gull, or I might find a very sharp-toothed little creature to bite you on the behind!'

'Oof,' said Patch, when they were safely out

in the street again, 'that was close. If Thomas hadn't been there, he'd have been *really* angry. You are an idiot, Pinch!'

'Idiot yourself,' said Pinch, sharply. He shot a glance at Thomas. 'Sorry. I didn't know it was going to streak out so quickly!'

'It's OK,' said Thomas. The flapdragon had surprised him, but it's hard to be really scared of something that smells like a Christmas pudding.

'Morph's the best Dream-maker ever,' said Patch, proudly.

Pinch growled, 'You always say that. But Dr Fantasos in Aspire is just as good. Even better! He's won more awards.'

'So what?' said Patch, hotly. 'He just stole most of Morph's ideas! He's Morph's cousin,' she told Thomas. 'He was supposed to be helping him in the workshop. But he left Morph and went over to Aspire when they said they'd give him a brand-new workshop of his own, built just exactly the way he wanted it!'

'Oh,' said Thomas. He was beginning to be rather curious about Aspire!

FOUR

They came to the next shop. This was Hinkypunk Hobthrust's Tricks For All Times. It was a small, dark shop, with a rather low door.

From his pocket, Pinch produced a tiny jar. 'Before we go in, I think you'd better have some of this.' He unscrewed the lid. Inside was a rather smelly green ointment.

Patch saw Thomas's expression. 'Don't worry, it's better than it looks! It's one of Mother's special mixtures. Repelling cream. Put some on your hands. Otherwise the tricks stick to you. Then they're really hard to shake off. And they can be really annoying.'

Thomas spread it on gingerly. To his

surprise, it went clear at once, and felt cool and tingly, and rather pleasant. The twins put some on too. Pinch put the jar away, and pushed open the door. A bell tinkled.

Inside the shop, a huge counter took up one wall. Shelves lined the others. Behind the counter sat a very elegant gentleman, writing in a large book.

'Good afternoon, Pinch, Patch and True Tom,' said the gentleman, in a silky sort of voice, not looking up from his work. He had gleaming red hair under a dark green, tasselled cap. He wore a smart green suit with a white flower at the buttonhole. His hands were small, very pale, and covered in gleaming red hair. He wore rings on his long, thin fingers, but the nails were black and curved, like talons.

'Good afternoon, Mr Hobthrust,' said Pinch in a rather nervous voice. 'We . . . we just brought Thomas to meet you and see your shop.'

'That's nice of you, Pinch,' said Hinkypunk Hobthrust. He looked up at Thomas. That narrow face, that sharp nose, those twitching whiskers, those yellow eyes, thought Thomas. Why, the Trickster looks just like a—

'Not a *fox*, Thomas, but a *Werefox*,' said the elegant gentleman, as if he could read Thomas's mind. He smiled, showing a mouthful of sharp, pointed teeth. 'Didn't Pinch and Patch tell you? How silly of them. Well, you are most welcome to my humble shop, Thomas.'

Thomas said, a little uncomfortably, 'Thank you, sir.'

Hinkypunk came out from behind the counter. There was something odd about the way he moved, as if he should really be running on four legs. He beckoned to Thomas. 'Come closer, let me show you some of my goods. This trick, for starters. We send it out into your world quite a lot.'

He reached a taloned hand into one of the

shelves. There was a sharp squeal. Suddenly, there was something in his hand. It was a long eel-like creature, which flashed with colours, like an oil slick. 'Meet the repeater,' said Hinkypunk. 'I believe you humans call it déjà vu.'

Without warning, Hinkypunk threw the repeater at Thomas. Before he could think, Thomas had grabbed it. As it touched his skin, it squealed, flipped over, and headed straight back to Hinkypunk, like a returning boomerang.

Hinkypunk caught the repeater. He stroked it, soothing it. He smiled in a rather disappointed way. 'You've got Old Gal's repelling cream on, Thomas! Well-prepared, you are. Well done.' He put the repeater back on the shelf, where it curled up and went to sleep.

Another quick grab, and in Hinkypunk's hand was a white blob that flopped about rather repulsively. 'Now this is a sock eater.

Every home in the Obvious World has got at least one of these beauties. They love living in the corner of Obbo laundry baskets. One of my new models, this one.'

He didn't try to throw it at Thomas, but put it carefully back.

'Usually,' he said, 'I work on my own. But sometimes, I join in with my friend Willy Wisp, next door. We make strange, tricky lights that lure travellers in deserted places in your world, Thomas, and make them go round and round in circles in fog, and at night. That can be quite fun.' Hinkypunk caught Thomas's shocked expression. 'Oh, it's nothing really bad. Nobody's died from it. I'm not a proper Uncouther, you know. The spells just send people a bit batty for a while.'

Thomas couldn't help a little shiver going up his spine as he looked into the Werefox's laughing, cold, yellow eyes.

'Tell Thomas about the anklebiters, Mr Hobthrust,' said Pinch, eagerly.

'Not much call for them these days, Pinch – not since those newfangled Obbo milking machines,' said Hinkypunk, smiling thinly, 'but I'll oblige.' He made a swoop at another shelf. There in his hand crouched a shabby little creature, human-shaped, but with a long tail, and a very odd face: tiny eyes and nose, and a huge mouth, full of needle-sharp teeth. 'I used to send these out into dairies, to nip at cows' legs and milkmaids' ankles,' said Hinkypunk. 'This is one of the few left. I haven't used one in years. Maybe I'll have to retrain it for some other job.'

'What about the tail-puller? The chair-disappearer?' gabbled Pinch. 'Or what about the—'

'Pinch,' said the Werefox calmly, 'you talk too much. Take a leaf out of your sister's book. Or perhaps you'd like to see my yallery again?'

'Oh, no. No thank you, Mr Hobthrust, sir,' said Pinch, backing quickly away. 'We'd best be going now, I expect.'

'Perhaps,' agreed the Werefox, grinning. 'Well, glad to meet you, True Tom the second. You're welcome any time you want to see my tricks. I've got lots more to show you!'

Out in the street again, Thomas said, 'What did he mean by not being a proper Uncouther?'

'He's got Uncouther blood, way back. Long ago, even before the war with the Uncouthers, an Uncouther girl married a Middler boy. Their children became the Tricksters. They create all the little mysteries and puzzles of your world.'

'Oh. Right. And what's a yallery? Why were you scared of it?'

Patch laughed. 'It's this horrible little thing that follows you around, repeating everything you say. Really loudly! It drives you mad. Hinkypunk set it on Pinch once.'

'Wasn't funny,' said Pinch, sulkily. 'I had to keep quiet for a whole week, until it got tired of following me around.'

'Oh, that was a blissful time,' said Patch.

Pinch made a face at her.

Back at the Apple Tree Café, the front door was wide open. A tall, thin woman with greenish skin, thin arms and a head of hair like a bird's nest was standing on the steps, chatting to Adverse Camber. She broke off when she saw the children.

'Oh, there you are! Honestly, Pinch and Patch, where have you been? I've been looking for you everywhere. You haven't finished your chores yet.'

'Mother, this is Thomas,' said Patch, hastily. 'He's our Rymer. We've been showing him around.'

'I see,' said their mother. She looked at Thomas, rather sternly. 'Pleased to meet you. I'm Old Gal Gull. I hope these two rascals of mine haven't been annoying you?'

'Oh, no!' said Thomas, eagerly. 'It's been fun, and I'm glad we—'

'Good,' broke in Old Gal briskly. 'I'm pleased. But now it's time Pinch and Patch came home, I'm afraid.' She turned to the twins. 'You'd better come right now and finish your chores. Or else there'll be all the cauldrons to scrub out as well.'

Pinch wailed, 'Oh, Mother! It's not fair! Can we see Thomas later?'

'Tomorrow,' said their mother, firmly, shepherding them out. 'Tomorrow, after breakfast, once you've done your chores, Thomas can come and visit you.'

They waved goodbye and left. Thomas and Adverse Camber watched them going up the street. Thomas said, 'She's a bit strict, their mum, isn't she?'

'Old Gal's a Solitary,' said Adverse. 'She's a fantastic herbalist, but she's rather fierce and proud, like all Solitaries. She keeps herself to herself, mostly, and doesn't join in village life much. The twins have been a bit bored and lonely. They'll be thrilled you're here now.'

Adverse clapped his hands and turned to Thomas. 'Right, young Tom. Come in and have a look at what your dad has done with the café!'

It looked wonderful. On each of the four walls was a big painting: of spring, summer, autumn and winter. They looked quite real, as if you could walk right into them. Tables with checked cloths and comfy chairs were scattered around. There was a gleaming wooden counter. Behind it were shelves stacked with jars of biscuits, of sweets, and brightly-coloured bottles of various drinks. Behind a glass display case were plates of cakes from the Zephyrus bakery. Delicious smells filled the air.

Thomas's father was busy at the counter. He looked different, somehow, and for a moment Thomas couldn't work out why. Then he realised. His father was happy, for the first time Thomas could remember.

'Hello, son,' Gareth said, smiling. 'How do you like it?'

'It's amazing,' said Thomas, truthfully. 'It's just . . . amazing.'

'When I was a little boy, I used to dream about having a shop like this. In fact, it was *exactly* like this. I'd even drawn a picture of it.' Gareth's voice became dreamy.

'Angelica Eyebright told me the café would be whatever I wanted it to be. And though I hadn't thought of it for years and years, those pictures came back into my mind, as fresh and sharp as when I'd drawn them. And here I am!' He pinched at his cheeks. 'I've been telling myself it's not real, but it doesn't go away.'

'It's real enough,' said Adverse Camber. 'You're in the Hidden World. This is where dreams come true, my friend.'

Gareth smiled. 'It'll take some getting used to. But it's wonderful. What about you, Thomas? What have you been doing?'

'Oh, all sorts of things!' said Thomas. 'I've

been in the bakery and the Dreaming Emporium and the tricks shop! But the best thing of all was meeting Pinch and Patch.'

Adverse Camber smiled. 'I'm sure it was. Now, just one small word of warning. You can explore as much as you want, in the village, up into the woods, wherever. Just stay away from the old mine-workings.'

In all the fun that morning, Thomas had quite forgotten the Uncouthers. Now he suddenly remembered them. But before he could speak, his father said, anxiously, 'Do you mean to say the Uncouthers could come up through an old mine?'

'Oh, no, no,' said Adverse, quickly. 'They can't. The mine-workings have all been quite filled in. Still, better to be safe than sorry, eh? Best not get about on your own too much, Thomas. Stick with Pinch and Patch, you'll be fine.'

Adverse turned to go. 'Oh. By the way, I actually came to tell you that Angelica's gone away. She's visiting the Montaynards. They're discussing re-forming the old alliance against the Uncouthers, just in case. She's taken Metallicus, and won't be back for a day or so. If you need anything, just come to me.'

He went out. Gareth looked at Thomas, the anxiety back in his face. 'I don't like it, I really don't. Oh, Thomas! You will be careful, won't you?'

'Don't worry, Dad. I don't want to meet the Uncouthers any more than you do. I won't go near the mine-workings, and I'll go everywhere with Pinch and Patch.'

Thomas spoke lightly, but all the same, he couldn't help feeling just a little uneasy. He hoped Adverse was right, and that everything *was* fine. Because he had absolutely no idea what he'd do, if ever the Uncouthers attacked.

FIVE

Thomas thought he'd never be able to get to sleep that night, but as soon as his head touched the pillow, the bed whispered to him, 'I'm taking you sailing on the storied sea,' and before he knew it, Thomas was sailing away, across a silver ocean on a white ship, towards a castle that glimmered in the distance.

He woke to bright sunshine. The dream had been glorious. He lay there feeling rested, relaxed and happy, and thinking of his mother, who had stayed in this very room. He had heard her silver flute, playing in his dream . . .

He got up out of bed, had a quick breakfast, then set off at once for Pinch and Patch's house. It was a rather shabby, rickety cottage, perched at the edge of the woods. Inside, there was a strong smell of herbs and spices.

The twins' mother was out, but Pinch and Patch were at the sink, washing up jars and bottles. 'Nearly finished,' said Patch, cheerfully, as Thomas came in. 'We thought maybe today we could take you down to the river.'

'There's a really good lookout where you can spy on Aspire, too,' said Pinch.

'Oh, who cares about Aspire?' snapped Patch.

'It's worth seeing,' said Pinch. 'And I bet Thomas would like to.'

'Yes. I would,' said Thomas, honestly. He added, 'Adverse said we could go anywhere. Except the old mine-workings. He seemed worried about them.'

Pinch and Patch looked at each other. 'Somebody once heard rumbles there,' said Patch slowly. 'But it's all been filled in since then. It's not likely they'd be able to come up that way.'

'Do you think they're going to attack?'

'We don't know,' said Pinch. 'Nobody does, really. There's been rumours. But not everyone believes them. The Aspirants certainly don't.'

'Oh, them!' said Patch, haughtily. 'They don't believe the rumours, because they think they are much cleverer than us, and that they have a better spy system.'

'Maybe they're right,' said Pinch.

Patch tossed her head, crossly. 'Are we going to go to the river, or not?'

Down at the river, the twins took Thomas to a lovely quiet spot near a clump of willow trees. The Riddle sparkled invitingly in the sunshine. Thomas took off his sandals and paddled. The water was beautifully warm. He thought about what the twins had said. They hadn't sounded worried. Perhaps he shouldn't worry, either.

'Look at me!' yelled Pinch, suddenly leaping off the bank. In midair he turned into a diving kingfisher with shimmering blue wings. 'And me!' yelled Patch, not to be outdone, snapping her fingers and turning into a big green frog that plopped with a loud croak into the water. Thomas laughed. He wished he could snap his fingers and turn into something else.

Pinch and Patch sprang back into their own shapes. Pinch was panting. 'Wow, I did it at last! I've been trying to do a kingfisher for weeks!'

'You're lucky. I wish I could do something like that,' said Thomas.

The twins looked at each other. 'Well, we're not allowed to teach you that kind of thing – but we could teach you little bits of magic, if you like,' said Pinch.

'We'd better ask Miss Eyebright first, when she gets back,' said Patch, firmly.

Pinch stuck his tongue out at her. 'You're such a goody-goody, Patch! Hey, Thomas, how about we go up to the lookout now?'

* * *

The lookout was actually a wooden platform in a tree, high up on the river-bank. From there, you could see quite a way over the other side of the Riddle, and to the far edges of the woods.

Aspire glittered in the middle distance, all glass and silver and white. Thomas said, 'Wow. It looks really different from Owlchurch.'

'That's what they want,' said Patch. 'They want to be modern. They think we're too old-fashioned.'

Her brother snorted. 'They could be right.'

'Pinch! What's the matter with you? How can you say that!'

'Quite easily. I don't like the Aspirants,' said Pinch, defiantly, 'but they might not be wrong about everything.'

'Oh, you're impossible, Pinch!' She pointed to a crystal dome in the centre of Aspire. 'See that place? That's Frosty's Café. It's horrid. Cold. Too neat. Not cosy and fun, like the Apple Tree.'

'But it has good food,' said Pinch, obstinately. 'I think we— Look, Patch!' he squealed. 'Look down there, at the bridge. Look who's coming!'

Thomas looked towards the bridge. A long, gleaming, white limousine, with a silver crest that flashed in the sun, was coming slowly over the bridge. Patch clutched Pinch. 'Hey! It's *them*! Lady Pandora and Mr Tamblin! I bet they've come to check out Thomas!'

'I bet they're going to try and poach him away,' growled Pinch.

Thomas laughed. 'Well, they won't,' he said. 'I won't let them. I like Owlchurch.' But I wouldn't mind seeing Aspire, he thought. Up close, not just from a lookout.

'Let's just stay up here,' said Pinch, gleefully. 'If they don't find you, Thomas, they'll look really stupid. They'll have made a trip for nothing.'

'Don't be silly,' said Patch. 'You knew it was bound to happen. The Aspirants were sure to find out Thomas is here, and want to meet him. Might as well get it over with.'

They scrambled down and raced along the river, back to the village. They were just in time to see the limousine draw up outside the Apple Tree Café.

The driver's door opened. The chauffeur stepped out. He wore a braided uniform, but instead of a chauffeur's cap, he had a magnificent pair of silver stag's antlers on his head, and an extra, pale-blue eye in the middle of his forehead. He opened one of the back doors. And out stepped two incredibly glamorous people.

First came a woman – slim, willowy and very beautiful. She was dressed all in cream: jacket, skirt and high-heeled shoes. Her hair was the colour of the ripest chestnut, and her eyes were bright green. Next was a tall, broad man, dressed almost completely in black – from his boots to the black ribbon, holding back his long black hair. Even his eyes were black. The only contrast came from his very pale skin and very red lips, and a cream-coloured cravat, with a silver crest printed on it.

They saw Thomas and the twins, and stopped. The woman drawled, 'Well, well, Pinch and Patch Gull! Perhaps you might introduce us to your friend.'

'This is Thomas,' said Patch, reluctantly. 'Thomas Trew. And this . . . this is the Lady Pandora and Mr Tamblin. They're the Mayors of Aspire.'

'Well met, Thomas Trew!' said Mr Tamblin, bowing. His smile didn't quite reach his eyes. 'We couldn't wait to see our new Rymer. It is a long time since—'

'He's *our* new Rymer,' broke in Pinch, hotly. 'You can't take him away from us!'

Mr Tamblin lifted a groomed eyebrow. 'Dear, dear. Who said we were even trying to?'

At that moment, the door of the Apple Tree burst open. Adverse Camber stood on

59

the doorstep, Gareth behind him. 'Lady Pandora, Mr Tamblin,' the dwarf said, coldly. 'What a surprise.'

'We've come to pay our respects to the Rymer, and bid him and his father most welcome,' said Lady Pandora, sweetly. She smiled at Gareth. It was a dazzling smile. 'And we've also come to ask if we may perhaps take him over to Aspire today, and show him around. We are neighbours, after all. Having a Rymer in the neighbourhood can only be a good thing for all of us.'

'We in Aspire are most conscious of the long friendship that has existed between the Rymers and our people,' said Mr Tamblin, smoothly. He shot a sharp glance at Adverse Camber. 'As you well know, in the past Rymers have lived in Aspire too. We never dreamed of keeping our Rymers to ourselves. We are happy Owlchurch is hosting this Rymer. We are not trying to lure him away. We simply ask that we be allowed to show a small token of our esteem. Mr Trew, would you allow your son to accompany us?'

'Well, I suppose there's no harm in it, is there?' said Gareth, appealing to the dwarf.

Adverse Camber shrugged. 'Suit yourself. It's up to you.' And he stomped off back inside the café.

The Lady Pandora laughed a tinkly laugh. 'Oh dear, I do fancy our Mr Camber doesn't approve of us. But we'll take good care of your son, Mr Trew, we do assure you. His mother came to visit us too. We took good care of her.'

'As long as he doesn't go near the mineworkings, I suppose,' said Gareth, lamely.

Thomas could see he was quite dazzled by Lady Pandora.

'The very idea,' said Lady Pandora, shuddering. 'Nasty dirty place. No, we will take him on a tour of our village, and he can have afternoon tea at Frosty's. We'll have him back here before nightfall. What do you think, Thomas?'

'OK, I'll come,' said Thomas, boldly, 'but only if Pinch and Patch can come too.'

Lady Pandora looked at the twins. An expression of distaste crossed her face. 'Very well. If they must.'

Pinch said, in a kind of strangled croak, 'I don't want to go.'

Thomas was astonished. 'But, Pinch, I thought you were all for—'

'I *don't want* to go!' shouted Pinch, and took off up the street. They all looked after him.

Mr Tamblin raised his eyebrows. 'Well, well, what's bitten him?' He turned to Patch. '*You're* not running away, too?'

'No,' said Patch, sharply. '*I'm* definitely coming.'

'Afraid we're going to steal Thomas away, are you?' Mr Tamblin's voice held a trace of bitterness. 'We're all on the same side, Patch Gull. Just remember that.'

As they got into the limousine, Thomas whispered to Patch, 'What's up with Pinch?'

'He doesn't trust 'em,' was her reply.

'But he said Aspire was worth seeing. I thought he'd want to come.'

'Well, he doesn't any more, does he? Maybe because they make him feel bad. They look at us as if we were worms. I don't care. But Pinch does.'

She relapsed into silence as Mr Tamblin and Lady Pandora got in beside them. 'Home, please, Herne,' said Mr Tamblin to the driver.

They came swiftly out of Owlchurch, and down the rather bumpy road that led to the Riddle Bridge.

Mr Tamblin shook his head. 'I'm afraid Owlchurch hasn't been looking after this road properly. These holes should have been mended.'

'They were!' said Patch, sharply. 'But then the road was damaged again. Maybe it's the Uncouthers moving underground.'

A glance flicked between Mr Tamblin and the Lady Pandora.

'Not *that* silly story again! Why, I believe it's just an excuse for shoddy work,' said the Lady Pandora lightly.

'Those rumours are quite untrue. The Uncouthers haven't been a problem in a long, long time,' said Mr Tamblin, smiling.

'But we heard—' Patch began.

'There are no holes in *our* village or on *our* side of the road, Patch Gull,' said Mr Tamblin. 'Owlchurch is just inventing excuses to make up for its own defects. The Queen of the Uncouthers would never break the treaty. You know that.'

Patch looked mutinous. 'The Queen might not be in charge any more!'

Lady Pandora laughed. 'Goodness me, now the child presumes to teach us politics! Of course the Queen's in charge. She always has been. The trouble with you Owlchurchers is that you listen to gossip and rumours.'

Patch said nothing more.

They reached the bridge. Halfway across, there was a locked double gate, with one gatekeeper guarding each side. The Owlchurch gatekeeper was a thin, pixie-like person with a cross face and suspicious eyes. But the Aspire gatekeeper was a tall, willowy girl with long silver hair to her waist and a sweet smile.

'Who's this? Who's this you've got with you?' growled the pixie, standing on tiptoes to peer through the open window of the car.

'Thomas Trew – our new Rymer – and Patch Gull,' said Mr Tamblin, lightly. 'They're on an official visit to us, Keeper.'

'Is that so?' said the pixie. He chuckled, coarsely. 'A Gull, on an official visit to Aspire! I've seen everything now, I have!' So saying, he unlocked his side of the gate, and stomped off.

The Aspire gatekeeper couldn't have been more different. She opened the gate at once, smiling. 'Welcome, dear visitors,' she fluted in a silvery voice. 'We hope your stay is a pleasant one.'

Thomas and Patch looked at each other. There was no need to say anything. The contrast was painful.

Aspire looked beautiful from the lookout, but up close it was breathtaking. Most of the glittering glass and metal and stone buildings were dome-shaped, with a few of a slender needle shape. Like Owlchurch, it was built around a central green.

The shops that lined the square were miracles of light and colour, and Frosty's made the poor old Apple Tree look pretty fusty. As to the village church, it was more like a small cathedral, all silver, white and crystal. A beautiful statue of an angel stood in front.

'The Light Angel, our patron saint,' explained Mr Tamblin. 'So, what do you think so far?'

'It's gorgeous,' breathed Thomas. Patch said nothing, but her face was full of light.

Mr Tamblin looked pleased. 'You see, the Hidden World must stay important to humans. Owlchurch still looks the way it did a hundred years ago, and it's out of date and crumbling. And spell-wise, well, Owlchurch still uses basically the same ingredients and formulas as it did back then. We've changed, created new things. And so, as you see, we're doing very well indeed. Why, just last year we hosted the biggest Convention of Master Magicians and Enchanters any of the worlds have ever seen!'

Before Thomas or Patch could respond, the car pulled up outside one of the buildings, a large dome of glass and silver, picked out with patches of striking black. 'We thought you'd like to start the tour with Dr Fantasos's Dream Boutique,' said Mr Tamblin.

SIX

Though Dr Fantasos was Morph Onery's cousin, the only family resemblance was the black skin and the two-coloured eyes. Dr Fantasos was as tall and graceful as Morph Onery was short and hunched, as serene as his cousin was explosive, as smart as Morph was untidy. The Aspire Dream-maker wore a beautiful pearl-grey suit, with a silver cape over his shoulders, and a black cravat. In his hand, he carried a small golden whip.

Bowing politely, he shepherded them into the first room in his vast emporium. It was large and bright, its walls seemingly made of liquid silver. 'This is our main production line,' he said, pointing with his whip. Thomas saw a bank of glass consoles, from which came a spider's web of fine silver wires. Rows of elegant Aspirants, dressed in pure white, sat at each console. Each of them held a line of wire and was working it in together with others, then connecting the joined wires to the consoles.

'We call it the Quicksilver Line,' said Dr Fantasos, happily. 'The dreams are not sent any old how, but are precisely targeted to particular kinds of people. Unlike my cousin's rather brainless Dream Flyers, each one of our Quicksilver workers understands the pattern of the dream and the dreamer. The dreams do not then run the risk of either clumping together in one place or drifting on the wind, to be lost. So these dreams feel very real – more real than Morph Onery's.'

Thomas watched the Quicksilver workers closely. As their nimble fingers worked at connecting the wires, he saw that something leaped between each of the lines, something bright and sharp and vivid. It made pictures flash in his mind. He saw himself and his father in Aspire. He saw Mr Tamblin and the Lady Pandora inviting him often to their lovely mansion, and eating the best, most delicious food with them. He saw himself dressed in perfect Aspire clothes, speaking in a perfect Aspire way; he saw himself growing up to be clever, bright, handsome and famous. He could see himself looking across the river at Owlchurch, and laughing at its ridiculous, old-fashioned ways. Then he felt himself being pulled towards the consoles, towards those Quicksilver wires. He felt, rather than heard, Patch's cry of alarm. He stepped back from the consoles. But not before he felt the icy burn on his skin as his thumb came close to the Quicksilver.

'Ow!' he yelled.

'Don't put your thumb in your mouth,' scolded Dr Fantasos. 'Go and get some ointment,' he added, turning to an assistant. 'And be quick about it.'

Neither Mr Tamblin nor the Lady Pandora had reacted to Thomas's misadventure. Indeed, they were smiling faintly.

Thomas caught Patch's eye. He was feeling a little cold, and a little hollow. The pictures he'd had in his head suddenly made him feel ashamed, and uneasy. Had the Aspirants intended to turn him against Owlchurch? Or was it just an accident?

Dr Fantasos took them into more production rooms, each filled with different ways of creating dreams. But now Thomas was wary. He saw with different eyes. He realised now that all the glamorous rooms, all the clever ways of sending out dreams, were *not* better than Owlchurch's, only *different*. And some of them weren't really that different at all. For example, there was a room like Morph Onery's dream zoo, filled with cages of little animals.

The cages were made of shimmering light and silver, and the creatures inside looked like holograms, but otherwise they were identical to the ones in Owlchurch.

It was obvious that Morph Onery's zoo had inspired it. So what were they boasting about?

The next shop they visited was that of the baker, Miss Ambergris. As they went in, Patch whispered to Thomas, 'I think Cumulus's place is much nicer!'

Thomas could only agree. There was none of the friendly, golden warmth of the Ariel's shop here. Miss Ambergris was the chilliest Aspirant they'd met so far, cooler even than the superior Lady Pandora. Her very skin was the colour of snow, her eyes paler than a winter sky, her hair the blue-white shade of ice, her wings sharp and pure white. Her cakes were arranged in strict rows, and all of them were white or silver, simply decorated. No twists, no turrets – and no steaming pies, either, no good smells, just a faint scent of some pale flower.

'Miss Ambergris makes the most elegant fare in all of the worlds,' drawled the Lady Pandora. 'She has distilled the essence of silver and the pure fragrance of cloud – the flavour enjoyed by angels. It has never been done before.'

Miss Ambergris did not smile at these compliments, though she inclined her head a little.

'Dear Miss Ambergris,' said Mr Tamblin. 'May Thomas taste one of your marvellous creations?'

Miss Ambergris fluted, 'A cake for the Rymer? Of course.'

'And for my friend,' said Thomas, boldly. Miss Ambergris's glance flew to Patch. If it were possible, her gaze seemed to get even cooler, her nostrils pinched. 'Angels' food is not for everyone,' she said, at last.

'Oh? Really?' Thomas began, hotly, but Patch nudged him.

'Don't be silly. It's probably not safe for me. But you can tell me what it's like.'

'The Gull child is right,' said Mr Tamblin, quietly. 'She is one of us, Thomas, remember – one of the Hidden World. There are rules here you don't understand yet.'

So Thomas took the tiny cake Miss Ambergris handed to him, and bit into it. It was lovely! He could hardly describe the taste, but it was delicious. 'It's very nice,' he said, when he'd swallowed the last mouthful. 'Really good.'

Miss Ambergris's cold face was suddenly lit by a dazzling smile. It didn't exactly warm her face but it suddenly made her look a lot nicer. She said, 'I know I'm not quite up to Cumulus's standards, but . . .'

'He is older than you,' put in Mr Tamblin, smoothly. But Miss Ambergris shook her head. 'He is a great master,' she said, 'and I admire him whole-heartedly. But I am glad you enjoyed it, Thomas.'

Why, she's really quite nice, thought Thomas, surprised.

'One more place to visit then, before lunch

at Frosty's,' said Mr Tamblin, smiling, as they made their way out into the street again. 'I rather think you'll like Monsieur Reynard's Institute of Illusion!'

It was a tall, needle-shaped building. At first glance it looked impossibly narrow, but, closer, suddenly it seemed to peel out and expand, like a flower emerging from a tight bud.

Inside was a great glass hall, with a silver desk exactly in the middle of it. A sleek Werefox sat there. He had shining, slicked-back silver hair, a pure-white suit, and yellow eyes in a narrow face. Just as Hinkypunk had the red look of a woodland fox, his counterpart in Aspire had the languid silver elegance of an Arctic fox.

'Monsieur Reynard,' said Mr Tamblin, 'allow me to present our new Rymer, Thomas Trew.'

Monsieur Reynard gave a thin smile. It showed his needle-sharp white teeth. 'Welcome! I am so glad to meet you.'

'We wish to show Thomas the Institute, and all the marvellous things you've done, Renny,' drawled Lady Pandora. 'He's only seen Hinkypunk's, you see.'

Monsieur Reynard shuddered, delicately. 'Oh, dear!' He picked up a glossy brochure lying on the desk, and handed it to Thomas. 'Some of our possibilities you might want to select . . .' he murmured, flicking at a non-existent speck of dust on his perfect suit.

Thomas opened the brochure. 'Perfect Illusions', it was called. The first picture was incredibly detailed – an underwater city complete with odd, fishy creatures swimming around, with bulging eyes, pin-stripe jackets out of which their fins flopped, and top hats. He touched the picture – and jumped back in alarm as his finger touched water, ripples of it swimming under his touch. He looked around him; the hall seemed to have disappeared. He was, indeed, swimming, floating in a strange, weightless sea. The others seemed to have vanished, except for Monsieur Reynard's mouth, full of sharp white teeth, and he heard Monsieur Reynard's silky voice, 'Turn, page, turn . . .'

The illusion melted into a shimmering mirage of desert, domes and cupolas, appearing above a golden, flowing ocean of sand. He felt the hot sun bearing down on his head, and in the distance, a group of fierce-faced men, swathed all in white, approaching at great speed on galloping camels . . .

'Turn, page, turn!' whispered Monsieur Reynard, and all at once, Thomas was in a dark wood, wandering on a narrow path.

At the end of the path, he could see a faint light, bobbing palely up and down, luring him on. Suddenly, Thomas felt Patch's hand on his arm. He knew the Middler child was trying to warn him. Something was wrong. But he couldn't stop himself. Something pushed him on. He wanted to know what was at the end of that path. He really, *really* wanted to know!

And so he kept walking, and the light kept bobbing away from him, just that little bit ahead. All at once, he stopped. He could see a house at the end now, a house made all of cake and biscuits and sweets, like a gingerbread house, its roof covered with tiles bright as icing sugar. It reminded him of something he'd seen in a book, but it was so much more real, and he felt so hungry! The door to the house was open, and in the doorway stood a kindly-looking old woman with white hair and bright, bright eyes. She was smiling at Thomas, beckoning, inviting him in.

Thomas took a step towards her – and at that very moment, the ground rumbled, gave way beneath him, and everything went black.

SEVEN

He came to a short while later. He was lying on something hard. It was still pitch black. His head hurt. What was happening? Then he remembered. He'd been in the Institute of Illusion, walking up to the gingerbread house! This must still be part of it. He waited for Monsieur Reynard to say 'Turn, page, turn.'

But instead, another voice spoke very close to his ear.

'He's coming round.'

It was a rough voice. A voice he'd never heard before.

'We'd better get him up,' said another voice,

rather squeaky this time. 'Himself will want to see him, for sure.'

'What do you think Himself will do?'

'Search me. But he must be a Middler spy. And if we let him go, they'll know, Up There, what we've been doing. Stands to reason we'll hold him. Sell him to Up There, maybe. Or maybe kill him.'

If this was an illusion, Thomas thought, he wanted Monsieur Reynard to stop it, right now. It wasn't fun any more.

He whispered, 'Please . . . please, turn the page . . .'

'Eh?' A light was struck, and two faces appeared at him out of the gloom – one large and broad, covered in warts, with not two but three eyes – two small piggy ones, and one like the eye of a crocodile, above a snout of a nose. The other was rather like a rat's, with a sharp, pointed snout, glittering red eyes, and sparse, stiff hair and whiskers. Both creatures wore iron helmets, tied under the chin.

They stared at him. Thomas stared back, unable to speak or move.

And then in the next moment, he nearly screamed, for something tiny, cold and wet had jumped into his hand. A faint whisper came to him. 'It's me, Patch. Put me in your pocket, carefully . . .'

'What are you doing, stranger?' said the broad-faced creature, peering suspiciously at him. Thomas slipped miniature Patch into his pocket and gulped, 'Nothing.'

'Get up, spy,' said the creature, prodding at him with something that looked horribly like a lance. 'We have to take you to Himself.'

'Yes, get up,' said the rat-creature, its eyes narrowed. 'We know you Up There are tricksy things, so don't think you can trick us, or you'll get what for.'

This is getting to be a bit too real, thought Thomas, struggling to his feet.

He could see the creatures better now. One was shorter, one taller than him, and they were both clad in leather and metal armour. One carried a lance, the other a short sword with a twisted blade. Their skin was a mottled grey-white, like things that have never seen the sun.

'Excuse me, but can you tell me where I am?' Thomas said, politely, hoping that if he spoke directly to them, the illusion would vanish. But nothing of the sort happened. Instead, the creatures started to laugh, a horrible sound. Then Rat-face spluttered, 'You Up There are

83

tricksy things indeed, pretending you don't know so you can use your magic on us!'

'You must be an illusion,' said Thomas desperately. 'You must be. Let me go, now!'

'Let you go? Certainly not!' yelled Broad-face, moving threateningly towards Thomas, who took a step back. 'Himself would have our guts for garters, you tricksy, Up There spy!'

Froggy Patch moved in Thomas's pocket. Her whisper came to him like a silver thread of sound. 'Careful, True Tom, they're Uncouthers. There's no telling what they might do!'

Thomas's heart raced. How on earth . . . ? The Aspirants had said there were no holes in their village for the Uncouthers to come up through. He'd definitely been in Monsieur Reynard's Institute of Illusion in Aspire. How *could* he be in the Uncouthers' country?

'We're not letting you go, no, sir!' repeated Broad-face. 'Not for all the riches of Up There.' His voice sounded rather wistful, as if he hoped Thomas might actually offer them a bribe.

'Shut up, fool,' said Rat-face. 'Course we're not letting him go. Himself'll give us a medal, bringing him an Up There spy. He must be spying on our tunnel.'

Tunnel? thought Thomas, glancing up. So that was it! They were building a tunnel under Aspire! Somehow there must be a weak point right there in Monsieur Reynard's shop, and that was why Thomas fell through. So much for the Aspirants! *They* were putting the Hidden World at risk!

Broad-face broke into his thoughts. 'Get moving,' he rasped, and pushed Thomas in front of him. 'Quick march!'

Thomas didn't argue. It was pointless. Rat-face was in front of him, Broad-face behind. He marched, or rather stumbled, on and on and on. The tunnel went on and on, smelling of must and very dark. He could hear the Uncouthers' heavy breathing. There was no other sound. Would the tunnel never end?

All at once Rat-face stopped. In front of him

was a great black stone, carved all over with strange symbols that shone in letters of fire. Rat-face touched the stone. The letters glowed and flashed. With a great, rending, grinding sound, the stone spun around twice, then split in half. The two halves opened, like the sides of a double door: and there was a doorway.

Beyond it was light and noise. And a strange smell: half burning, half the dark stink of trapped, underground water. Thomas stopped, his heart beating fast, his hands clammy.

'In you go,' said Broad-face, pushing him roughly through. 'And take care you don't try your tricks on Himself, or not even your best, Up There magic will save you then!'

EIGHT

He was in a large cave, lit by flares. It was full of people – some dressed like Broad-face and Rat-face in soldiers' gear; others in glittering bits and stuff that looked like they were dressed for a party. Some were like Rat-face and Broad-face. Some of them were as elegant as the Aspirants. All of them, though, had that sunless skin.

In the centre of the cave gleamed a dark pool. Beside it rose a massive iron throne, at least three metres tall. The man sitting on it was a giant. His head easily reached the top of the throne. His massive hands, resting on the iron throne-arms, were half the size of

Thomas's head. His mailed feet looked as if they could just stamp the life out of you. He wore red and black armour, with a lightning flash on the breast. His hair was the burning colour of molten metal and his eyes were the pitch-black of the dark pool.

Beside him, on a low stool, sat the strangest-looking person. He was something like a tortoise (with a craning head and a humped back) and something like a monkey (with quick, darting hands, and quick, darting eyes). He wore a brown and silver uniform. There was a large, leather book perched on his knees, and a quill in his hand.

All eyes were on Thomas. His pulse beat wildly in his throat. Froggy Patch was absolutely quiet and still in his pocket, as if she were a stone. He knew he must not show that she was there.

Broad-face and Rat-face pushed Thomas to the ground. Then they too fell on their knees.

'Your Magnificence, we found this Up There

spy creature in the tunnel,' stammered Broad-face, nervously.

'He must have been poking around, Your Wonderfulness,' squeaked Rat-face. 'We acted very quickly, Your Gorgeousness, to bring this enemy spy to your hall.'

The Uncouther Lord said nothing. Thomas could feel the dark eyes resting on him. He smelled again that odd stink. The tortoise-monkey person was watching him very curiously indeed. So were all of the people in that hall.

At last, the giant spoke. He did not have the deep, booming voice Thomas had expected. It was rather light and toneless.

'How did he come here?'

It was a simple question but Thomas could see Rat-face and Broad-face shivering with fright. He raised his own eyes to the giant's face. There was no expression in the eyes at all.

'Well, Numbers 22AZ and 56T? I'm waiting.'

Broad-face looked like he was almost dead with fright. It was Rat-face who answered, in a tiny voice, 'Those Up There are so tricksy, my Lord. They can do things we—' He broke off, suddenly, eyes bulging with fright.

'Number 56T,' said the giant, 'why do you

not finish your words? Surely you do not mean to suggest that those creatures Up There are cleverer than we are? You, who come from the great city of Pandemonium, from the Land of Nightmare, dare to think this?'

'No! No, Your Gloriousness, Your Ironheartedness, I do not, no indeed.' Rat-face was shrunk into himself, his whole body shaking with fear, great gobs of sweat like big tears breaking out all over his dull skin.

Thomas had had quite enough.

'I fell through,' he said, getting to his feet. 'I was in the Institute of Illusion in Aspire, walking down a path to a gingerbread house, and I fell through.'

Everyone in the hall froze. For what seemed like an eternity, the giant stared unblinkingly at Thomas, searching his face.

'You're *not* a Middler!' said the Uncouther Lord, at last. 'And I don't think you're an Ariel, or a Montaynard, or one of the Seafolk. You're not from *any* race of the Hidden People. You must be an Obbo. Yet the Middlers have sent *you* as a spy. Why?'

A rustle went through the hall at these words.

'I am *not* a spy!' cried Thomas, hotly. 'I just fell through!'

The giant turned to the creature at his feet. 'Fustian Jargon, what is your learned opinion?'

The tortoise-monkey's mouth twisted – in amusement, it seemed. Its glittering eyes flashed. 'My Lord General,' it said in a voice as squeaky as Rat-face's, 'I think it is not from this world, as you so perceptively deduced.'

'Yet surely very few from the Obvious World can survive Pandemonium unscathed. And this one has not only survived, he dares to speak.'

'Yes, my Lord General.'

'Write, Fustian. Write that this Obvious creature has come into Pandemonium unscathed. Write that he dared to speak to me.' He paused. A hard glitter came into his cold eyes. 'Write that he *could* be a magician, a sorcerer come to learn from us. We have had such guests before. But I do not think so. He is too young. There is no darkness clinging to him. Write that therefore, he must be the human thing I've been looking for. He must be the Rymer!'

'Oh, my Lord General!' Fustian Jargon chattered with delight. His quill flew busily across the page. The crowd leaned forward, murmuring, staring at Thomas.

Fear made Thomas's knees knock, but he managed to hold his head high as he said, 'Sir, I don't know who you are, but you'd better let me go. My friends won't let you harm me – whoever you are!'

There was a gasp. The giant's eyes flashed, and narrowed to angry slits.

'How dare you, Rymer! Know that I am the only, the great General Legion Morningstar, Crown Prince of Pandemonium and all the Land of Nightmare, only son of the Queen Lilith Morningstar, Wearer of the Iron Crown of Nightmare. Soon, very soon, I will be absolute ruler in all this land, and then of the lands above.' He waved a hand. 'Write, Fustian Jargon! Write: that this Obbo slave dared to pretend not to know my name!'

'Yes, my Lord General,' said the little secretary, his eyes glinting even more with glee as his quill scratched out the words.

Thomas suddenly felt furious. 'Why should I know your name?'

'You have seen my city in your nightmares,' said Legion Morningstar, quietly, leaning towards Thomas. 'Like all Obbos, Rymer or not, you have sampled the dark bitterness of our land. You are bound to us. Now, Rymer, you must tell me your name.'

As if hypnotised, Thomas looked back into the blank dark eyes. At once, all the nightmares he'd ever had came flooding over him. He felt weak. His limbs shook. His teeth chattered. He could feel the General's dark power reaching into him, groping, trying to eat him, tunnelling into his mind, his heart, his soul. It was a huge force pulling at him, sucking him in . . . He couldn't resist. He couldn't!

Then, quite suddenly, a clear picture of his mother came into Thomas's mind. She looked pretty, and young, her hair long and flowing. Her brown eyes were full of love. He could hear her silvery flute-music in his head. It spoke of sunshine and warmth, tenderness and joy. It seemed to push back the darkness, to flood Thomas with a new strength, and new knowledge.

With a huge effort, he tore his eyes away from the giant's face. He felt sick and dizzy, but managed to croak, 'I will *not* tell you my name. All you need to know is that I am a Rymer, General Morningstar. And you can't hurt me, not here, in this world!' Was that true? He very much hoped so.

The General smiled, very nastily. 'Can't hurt you? No matter. *"Not hurting you"* could mean a variety of things. Isn't that so, Fustian?'

'Yes, my Lord General.' The little secretary licked his lips. 'It means he may not be molested. It means he can move through Pandemonium. But it certainly does not mean we have to let him go.' He paused. His eyes glittered. 'My Lord, you know we were a little concerned that his presence in Owlchurch might upset our plans . . . We thought of nightmaring him in his world before he came to the Hidden World. The Middlers got there before we could try. But now – well, he's fallen into our hands. We could *keep* him *here*. A permanent guest of Pandemonium. A Rymer in the Land of Nightmare. We need to know his name, but we will learn that soon enough, if he stays with us.'

'Ha! Has this ever been done before, Fustian?'

'No, my Lord General. But that does not mean it cannot be done. There is nothing in any of the rules expressly forbidding such a course of action.'

Thomas had been listening to all this with growing fear. 'You can't do that!' he cried desperately. 'I *won't* stay here! You have to let me go! Or my friends will come and get me, and then you'll be in deep trouble!'

The General ignored him. 'Write, Fustian Jargon. Write: that I, General Legion Morningstar, Bright Hope of the Worlds, have hereby conceived a most clever policy, which will see me hailed as a great hero. Write: we aimed to break into the Middler lands through the weak point under Aspire. But this is much better. Leave the tunnel. The Rymer will stay here. We will learn from him all we need to know to become the masters of the Hidden World. Write: long ago, his Rymer ancestor helped to defeat us. Well, we will use *this one* to defeat them up there! What a sweet revenge that will be! Now, Rymer, for the last time – tell me your name!'

Thomas shouted, 'No! No! I won't do it! You'll learn nothing from me! Nothing! I'll never, ever tell you anything – not my name, nothing!'

'That's what you think,' said the General, quietly. 'You don't know much about us, yet, Rymer. But you will. You will.'

He signalled to two burly, tiger-faced soldiers. 'Escort him to the guest chamber. And don't even think you can escape,' he went on, turning to Thomas. He gestured at the dark pool at his feet. 'Only the underground river leads out of here, and you cannot survive it, Rymer or not. Only the Hidden People can.'

Thomas stared at the pool. A wild idea leaped into his mind. Falling on his knees beside the pool, he cried, 'General Legion Morningstar, don't do this! Let me go! If you don't, my friends will hear about it, and they'll come to get me!'

Patch, he thought with all his might, hoping she had heard, and understood. Patch, the pool! You can do it! You can! It's our only chance! He felt a movement in his pocket, and bent down further to hide her from them. 'Please, my Lord General,' he said brokenly, 'please, let me go . . .'

A tiny flop. She was out. He alone heard the faint splash she made as she jumped into the pool.

'Write, Fustian Jargon,' said the General in a voice full of triumph. 'Write: the Rymer is a coward, afraid for his own skin. Write: that this is an insult to the great and noble lineage of Legion Morningstar, Crown Prince of Nightmare. Write: that this Rymer had better learn some manners, for he will be a long time in Pandemonium. Write: that we will now go to speak on this matter to our mother, Lilith Morningstar, Queen of Nightmare. Now, 433QY and 666TG, take this creature to the guest chamber.'

Thomas was hauled roughly to his feet and bustled out of the hall, dozens of pairs of mocking eyes on him. He tried to hold on to the thought of Patch, swimming through the underground river. Please be quick, he thought. Please, *please* be quick.

NINE

Thomas was led down great dark corridors. Their rocky walls were honeycombed with countless smaller tunnels which seemed to lead to actual dwellings. It was as if he and his guards were walking down the middle of great dark streets, lined with unending blocks of flats. This was Pandemonium: a city built into the black rock, a place where the sun never shone. But there were flickering lights in most of the dwelling-holes, and occasionally a curious, pitiless face peered at him from the passages.

His escorts did not speak to him, and he did not try to speak to them. His heart felt very heavy. The further they went down these corridors, these dark streets, the further they were getting from the place where he'd first landed. How would anyone ever find him here?

At last, the soldiers stopped. They had come to a central square. Around the square were several doors cut into the rock, much larger openings than those in the dwellings Thomas had seen along the way. Above the doorways were signs in twisted writing. They were quite unlike the jolly names of Owlchurch, or the elegant ones of Aspire. 'Commissar of Nightmares'; 'Night Terror Branch'; 'Factory of Mayhem', were just some of them.

In the very centre of the square was a big windowless building, whose walls were covered by huge portraits of Legion Morningstar, and of a beautiful, cold-eyed, silver-haired woman wearing a huge iron crown, who must be Queen Lilith. Beside it was a guard post.

The soldiers, still without speaking, took

Thomas to the guard post. It was a shabby, dark little room. A tall thin soldier with a fishy face sat at a desk. On the wall, an enormous portrait of the General frowned down at them.

Fish-face had a ledger opened in front of him. He barked, without looking up, 'Name, profession, date of birth. I will tell you date of death.'

'This is the Rymer, fool, not one of your ordinary charges,' said one of Thomas's escorts. 'He's to go to the guest chamber. Unlock the door.'

Fish-face looked up. His eyes were pure white, as if they'd been boiled. It was a horrible sight. 'A Rymer, eh?' he hissed. 'Haven't had one of those before.'

'I told you, he's not for you or your kind, fool,' said the soldier, harshly. 'He's not to be hurt.'

Fish-face smiled, revealing a row of needle-sharp teeth. He hissed, 'What does this mean, friend? Many things to many kinds.'

'I'm not your friend. And the Rymer's protected by the General himself, so you'd better watch out.'

'Oh, that I will,' said Fish-face, licking thin blue lips. 'That I will.' The boiled eyes looked at Thomas, who could not help shuddering. 'Welcome, guest,' the creature hissed. 'We hope you will be long with us.'

He got up. Selecting a tiny black key from a bunch around his waist, he went straight to the portrait of the General. He inserted the key into the lightning-symbol on the armour. At once, there was a click, the portrait swung back – and there, revealed, was a doorway. Not a dark, grim-looking one, but one decorated with red and gold designs. Golden-warm light, like a bit of trapped sun, flooded in.

Fish-face snarled, 'Nice, eh, Rymer? Lucky you are. Lucky. Sad me, not being able to write your name in my torture ledger. But perhaps later, eh? Perhaps later.' His hissing voice was full of hope.

* * *

Thomas stepped into a large, light, comfortable bedroom, lined with bookshelves crammed with books. What was more, it had a window! True, it was barred, but it was still a window. And through it, he could see a peaceful, sunny scene: water-meadows, with cows grazing, and a little house in the distance. It looked very cheerful. Thomas's spirits lifted. He hardly noticed the soldiers leaving the room, or the click of the lock behind them.

He went straight to the window and put his hand on one of the bars. At once, the scene shifted, shook, disappeared. He took his hand away. It came back. It was a trick! The window was a cruel illusion! Of course! How could he ever have thought it would be anything else?

He rushed for the door. He rattled the handle. But it did not budge. He was locked in.

Desperately, he shouted, 'Let me out! Let me out!'

All at once, there was a rustle at his feet; a

thin, timid voice somewhere near him. 'Rymer, you stop . . .'

Startled, Thomas looked down. A thing rather like a little bat crouched at his feet. It had tattered, folded wings rather like a broken umbrella, red, darting eyes, and wore a ragged black robe. It was bowed under the weight of an enormous tray. On the tray were a covered dish and a bottle of some dark liquid.

'This for you,' said the creature. 'You eat, drink.' It put the tray down on the floor.

'I'm not hungry,' said Thomas, turning his head away.

'If you not eat this, you die. You get sick here, very quick. Your blood, it freezes.' The creature looked up at him, its nose twitching. 'Is true you a Rymer?'

'Yes.'

'I heard, but never met. Never a Rymer here before as guest.'

Thomas said nothing. He had no interest in conversation. But the little creature persisted. It seemed eager to talk. 'Now Rymer come, things better. You stay.'

'No,' said Thomas, angrily. 'I am not staying. My friends will come and get me!'

'You stay,' said the creature, stubbornly. 'You eat. We help.'

This time, Thomas looked more closely at the thing. The expression in its eyes was – not exactly kind, but a little warmer than any others he'd seen here. He said, cautiously, 'How will you help?'

'You will see, Rymer. You stay. We help.'

Thomas gave up trying to convince the stubborn creature. 'What's your name?'

'Me called Guesty. On account of being guesthouse servant variety. But supposed to be slave 7777AZT, in new system devised by Lord General.'

Pity washed over Thomas. 'You're a slave?'

'No, no,' howled Guesty. 'I a *servant*! This not same!'

'All right, all right,' said Thomas, hastily. At least it was vaguely friendly. He couldn't say that about anybody else he'd met in Pandemonium so far.

'Give me this food, then,' he said. 'I might as well eat.' And indeed, he was suddenly very hungry.

Surprisingly, the food wasn't bad, though it was simple: hot bread and salty white cheese. The drink turned out to have a taste rather like cola. Guesty watched him eagerly as he ate, occasionally nodding its head and muttering things like, 'That bread, that good. Made by friend in Dagon's bakery . . . Rymer, he like . . . that one cheese, that from underground fish-cow in river . . . she have strong blood, that one, protect against darkness . . . good for Rymer . . .' and so on, more of the same. Thomas listened with only half an ear.

When he had finished, the creature grabbed the tray. 'Now Guesty go away. Will come back,' it added, hastily. 'Come back soon. There be festival here tonight. Rymer must know what to do.'

'I don't want to go to any festival . . .' began Thomas. But he was speaking to the empty air. Guesty had vanished.

Left alone, Thomas sat on the bed, his mind whirling. He couldn't even begin to imagine how to get out of this place. He could only hope that Patch would get back safely to

Owlchurch. And that his friends could rescue him! The Uncouthers had never had a Rymer here before. Maybe that would work against them. Or maybe not. Who knew what the rules really were, in this strange world? He certainly had no idea. What if he was stuck here for ever?

No, he wouldn't think about that! He wouldn't! He got up, restlessly. He looked around him. He went over to the bookshelf. From a distance, the books had looked different. Close to, Thomas saw that though they had slightly different titles, they were all by the same author: General Legion Morningstar, as written down by Fustian Jargon.

Thomas slid one out from the shelves. He opened it. No pictures coming to life here, and no story. Just boasting and boring speeches, on and on. He flipped the pages. More of the same dull, dull stuff, in cramped black script; but with, here and there, a passage written in what looked suspiciously like blood. Thomas looked closer. The hair rose on the back of his neck as he read. 'When I am master of the Hidden World and all the worlds above,' wrote the General, 'I will make such terrible nightmares that they will make the heads of human beings explode! I will make such terrors that their blood will turn to ice, and the darkness will reach up and swallow them whole, and grind their bones and their flesh! And I will laugh, and laugh, and be glad! For only Nightmare will rule, and Pandemonium silence everything!'

Thomas threw the horrid book across the room. His stomach was churning with fear and fury. He must stop the Uncouthers! He must! But how? How?

The image of his mother had helped him, back in the hall. Maybe it would again? He tried to call it up. But his mind stayed quite blank. There was no flute-music in his head. For the first time, he felt real despair. He wished he'd never seen any of the Hidden People. He wished he was back in London, in his grey house in his grey street on a grey afternoon. He put his head in his hands, and cried.

TEN

Suddenly, the door crashed open. Guesty was back. It was not alone. The creature with it had thin prehensile arms, short legs, feet like big broad flippers, and a long spiky tail. Its skin was bronze – not grey like the other Uncouthers – its bulging eyes golden. It wore a tight red and gold diver's suit. In one hand it carried a small package.

'Name's Salmagundo Firewalker,' it hissed. 'Deepfire diver, and spymaster to Queen Lilith.'

Thomas stared, sniffing a little. 'Deepfire diver? What's that?'

'I walk in Deepfire and gather new Murae slaves to work in the nightmare mills,' said

Salmagundo. 'I am under the direct command of Queen Lilith. I have been sent personally by her Gracious Majesty. Tonight is the Festival of Deepfire. The General believes that our people will find the surest path into the world above if a creature neither of the Hidden nor of the Obvious World falls into Deepfire. A magician would have done. But a Rymer is even better. We have heard whispers that this may be what our beloved General has in mind for you.'

Thomas's heart pounded. 'What do you mean? He wants to keep me prisoner here to learn from me! He's not allowed to hurt Rymers!'

'Oh, he can learn from you very well this way,' said Salmagundo Firewalker, smiling rather horribly. 'And he wouldn't directly hurt you, you understand. Easy for you to fall in accidentally, what? A sudden breath of wind, perhaps, a little quake, and you'd stumble into Deepfire. The General thinks that then your

power would give him an immense new energy, with which he would be invincible.'

A finger of cold tweaked Thomas's spine. He quavered, 'Why are you telling me this?'

'Queen Lilith is sure that this plan is far too dangerous. She thinks it would destroy the Land of Nightmare itself. She's looked the other way while he makes preparations for war, because she doesn't like the treaty any more than he does. She was quite happy about the idea of having you here, as well. A Rymer could be very useful to us. But this new plan is very dangerous, and going much too far. And so we are prepared to help you, Rymer. This is a great honour for you.'

Thomas's heart beat fast. 'What must I do?'

'You must take this, and put it on.' Salmagundo Firewalker unwrapped the package he was holding. In it was a thin strip of shiny material similar to the kind the Firewalker was wearing. 'This talisman is made of Deepfire-salamander skin, like my suit. Put it on once the ceremonies begin. With it on, you can survive a fall into Deepfire, as long as you don't fall too far. You should avoid going near it, in any case. And you are not to approach Her Majesty, and must remain silent on how you obtained this. All the time you are here, you must not approach her.' His voice was cold and indifferent.

Thomas could have slapped him. He shouted, 'Don't worry! I won't! And I won't stay here in this horrible place, either! I won't!'

Salmagundo Firewalker shrugged. 'You have no choice on that. You're here. Here you stay. But you do have a choice on Deepfire. You must take it, or the consequences are likely to be very grave for us.'

'And what about for me?' cried Thomas, angrily.

'Exactly,' said Salmagundo, and his weird face creased into a smile. 'We understand each other perfectly.' And ducking a little mocking bow, he was off.

'He is right,' said Guesty, nodding. 'You must do as he says. He is a great one, and close to Her Majesty. You stay. You already make things better. Salmagundo Firewalker, he not talk to me before; now he does.'

'I don't care!' said Thomas, furiously. 'I'm going, do you hear? My friends are coming to get me!'

Guesty shook its head. Its eyes were suddenly full of malice. 'How can you? No one know you are here. Tunnel been blocked up now. And you cannot go through Black Pool.'

It was on the tip of Thomas's tongue to boast about Patch. Luckily, he stopped himself. He said, sulkily, 'Go away and leave me alone.'

'No,' said Guesty. 'You not know anything. You must listen.'

Thomas kept his head turned away, and said nothing.

'When Queen Lilith in proper charge,' went on Guesty, stubbornly, 'things better than now. We servants, yes, but not *slaves*. Slaves only in mills and in mines. We *servants*. We have own place. Now she gives General her son more power, and he begins to change many things. He want to make nearly all slaves. This not good.'

Thomas said nothing.

'General is clever, but forget we his people. Think all are slaves. This bad! We better than those in mines and mills.'

'It's bad to have slaves anyway,' said Thomas, goaded. 'You only care about yourselves.'

'Those in mines and mills, always slaves! They Murae! You must understand! We different.'

'Why?'

Guesty stared at him. 'Because . . . this always so,' it said at last.

'If you all joined up together,' said Thomas, 'you could beat the General. There's only one of him.'

Guesty stared at him. Then it began to laugh; a horrid, discordant sound. 'You not understand anything! He is General Legion Morningstar, Crown Prince, heir of the Iron Crown. He is our Lord. Without him, without the Family, there would be nothing. You are Rymer, but you are fool. Besides, how can we join with Murae slaves? They not even speak. They have not even mouths. They be blind, deaf, dumb. They not even think. They only for work. Endless work. That is all they be.'

'They're machines?' said Thomas, his skin crawling. 'Robots?'

'What these? They be Murae, from Deepfire. They be slaves, always making nightmare. That their being! That is them. But we be not slaves, not Murae! We be servants. We be citizens of Pandemonium.'

'So what do you want? I don't understand.'

'A change back to old ways. You stay,' said Guesty, firmly. 'You put on salamander talisman.'

And before Thomas could say anything more, it had whisked out of the door, leaving him standing there with his palms clammy and his heart beating so fast he thought it might burst out of his chest. Oh, Patch, he thought, desperately. Patch, what's happened to you? Please, please hurry up!

ELEVEN

Yes, what had happened to Patch? For her, hitting the Black Pool had been like hitting a glass wall would be for a human – possible, but dangerous. The black shards of water flew perilously around her as she plunged into the Uncouther depths.

It was lucky she had practised her frog-morphing so often, and lucky she had chosen such a tiny shape, because she was able to dodge in and out of great splinters of nightmare that would have skewered something just a little bit bigger. But she wouldn't last long in there. She must find the hole in the wall where the underground river began. The water swirled and boiled around her. She could hardly see a thing. She was beginning to feel breathless and tired. Suddenly, she spotted it! She slid thankfully into it, and fell down a long dark tunnel, rushing with water. She paddled furiously.

The river fed into a notorious waterhole some distance from Aspire. It was not a place people liked to go near, because it was the home of a dangerous Solitary named Peg Powler. Peg protected the opening against Uncouthers. They wouldn't dare come up this way. But she was also rather unpredictable. Still, there was no help for it. Maybe, thought Patch, hopefully, Peg might be asleep.

Patch popped up like a cork into the open air. She was in the middle of the brackish pool. Without stopping to catch her breath, she immediately struck out for the bank. But she didn't get very far. A bony hand grabbed her froggy shape by the leg. In an instant, she was dangling centimetres away from a set of very sharp, very large green teeth, sprinkled with yellow scum.

Patch yelled, 'Peg Powler, let me go!'

There was a watery chuckle. A sweet voice emerged horribly from between the green teeth. 'Oo-er. A dear little sweetie talking froggy! Yum! Yum! What a nice little treat!' The teeth came closer.

Patch shrieked, 'Let me go! I'm the daughter of Old Gal, who will take vengeance on you if you hurt me! She'll make a mixture that will turn your insides out, and make all your teeth fall out!'

'Old Gal!' said Peg Powler, in a wary tone of voice, and dropped Patch with a splash.

Immediately, Patch changed back into her own shape. She swam with all her might to the bank, scrambled out and shook herself. She looked back. Peg Powler, with only her ugly head visible above the water, was ·watching her. She had wrinkled grey skin, hair that looked and stank like dead waterweed, and squinty eyes. She called out, in her horribly sweet voice, 'Oo-er, why did darling dearie Old Gal send her sweetie-pie of a daughter in delicious froggy form into my humble home?'

'She doesn't know about it,' said Patch, and fled. That was a close call, she thought as she ran, and no mistake. Lucky Mother has such a fierce reputation!

She was soon in Aspire. Ignoring curious stares, she ran as fast as she could to the Institute of Illusion, but a sign on the locked door proclaimed it to be 'Closed'. She went to Dr Fantasos's place, but that was also 'Closed'. Miss Ambergris's bakery was equally 'Closed'. Patch hopped about on one foot, trying to think. What about Frosty's? She ran there, but the place was shut and empty. She rushed around in the street, pulling at people's sleeves, asking them where the mayor of Aspire and his lady could be found, but to no avail. They just stared at her curiously, lips curled, and turned away. Snobs! she thought, angrily. It's their fault Thomas vanished, and they can't even be bothered to help me! She had to get back to Owlchurch as quickly as she could.

She didn't head for the bridge. That would take too much time. Instead, she went straight to the river, turned into a frog and jumped in. She paddled rapidly down the stream. And there was Pinch, sitting in their usual place, on the opposite bank. He was sulkily swinging his legs in the water, singing a cross little song to himself. He broke off when he saw the frog. He knew at once it was his sister.

'Where have you been?' he shouted, as Patch changed back into her own shape. 'Where's Thomas? You're in big trouble, you know!'

Patch glared. 'What do you mean, trouble?'

'Angelica Eyebright is back. She isn't happy that you went with Thomas to Aspire. Where *is* he?'

'The Uncouthers have got him! In Pandemonium! We've got to get him out of there!'

'What?' Pinch stared at her. 'Have you gone mad?'

'No time to explain,' said Patch. 'Come on!'

Angelica Eyebright was sitting at a table with Gareth Trew. She frowned when the twins came rushing in.

'So, Patch Gull, you're back! You—'

Patch broke in, desperately. 'Miss Eyebright! It's Thomas! He needs our help!'

Gareth Trew jumped up. 'Where is he?'

Patch explained, rapidly. When she'd finished, Gareth cried, 'I don't understand. Are the Aspirants in league with the Uncouthers?'

'Of course not,' snapped Angelica Eyebright. 'They might look down on us, but they'd *never* join with the Uncouthers. They know very well that the Uncouthers would destroy Aspire every bit as much as Owlchurch. No. Reynard must have some new illusion in his box of tricks that is much too close to real nightmare, and which made the patch of ground beneath his institute thinner than it should be.'

Patch nodded. 'It was the honey trap of a wicked witch.'

'By the horns of Pan, those Aspirants must be crazy! Still, we're going to have to ask them for help. We need our combined powers. No time for rivalries now. Now then,' went on Angelica, briskly, 'we need to move, and fast. Pinch and Patch, run and fetch Adverse Camber, Calliope Nightingale, Hinkypunk and Morph Onery. We'll go to Aspire. From there we'll go straight into Nightmare, through the honey trap. And we must be quick. I think it's the Festival of Deepfire tonight. Nightmare will be at its strongest, and we will not be in our own land.'

'I'm coming too,' said Gareth, firmly.

'No! We don't know how long it's going to take to get Thomas out of their clutches. You won't survive more than a minute or two in Uncouther country. The atmosphere of Nightmare would explode your brain.'

Gareth cried, 'But then Thomas . . .'

'He's a Rymer, it's different for him. He will not die there.'

Maybe not die, thought Patch, but they might keep him there, for ever . . . It had never happened before, but it might. They were in uncharted territory. Who knew what might happen?

'But I can't just stay here and do nothing!' wailed Gareth.

'No, I know you can't. That's why I'm asking you to help defend Owlchurch. It will be in danger while we're away. You must go to Cumulus and tell him the Defence Plan is to be activated at once. Tell him you are second in charge.' Angelica paused. 'Will you trust me with your son's safety, as I am entrusting you with the safety of Owlchurch?'

Gareth looked suspiciously at Angelica Eyebright. Then, slowly, he nodded.

TWELVE

Thomas could hear drums beating. His heart beat in time with them. The Uncouthers were getting ready for their festival. How long would his friends take?

He thought of the salamander talisman, now in his pocket. Even though he had no intention of going anywhere near the Deepfire, it was better to be safe than sorry. He didn't know exactly what Deepfire was, but he could guess. Some pit full of fire, maybe a crack into the deepest molten core of the earth, where only fire existed. Whatever, it wasn't good.

He roamed around the room, trying to find a way of getting out. But the room was tightly sealed. Whenever he touched the window, it disappeared, as before. The door was firmly locked. It was hopeless, and very soon he gave up. He stretched out on the bed. Time passed slowly and painfully. Nobody came to see him.

He was nearly asleep when the door burst open, and two soldiers came in. 'You come now,' said one. For a moment, Thomas thought of ducking under their arms through the doorway and making a dash for it through Pandemonium. But he'd never find his way out. So he followed them meekly out of the guest room, through the guard post where Fish-face stared hungrily at him, and into the dark laneways of Pandemonium.

They were very crowded now. The soldiers carved a way through. Thomas tried not to look to right and left as they passed, because when he did, all he could see were eager, cruel faces staring at him with the same hungry look as Fish-face. These people would have no mercy, he thought, no pity. In fact they probably wouldn't know what the words even meant. They would probably enjoy it if he was cast into Deepfire.

All the way along, Thomas could hear the drumming. It echoed in all the laneways and passageways of Pandemonium. As they went along, the drumming got louder and louder, the crowds thicker and thicker. At last, they reached a place like a huge arena, or stadium. It was floored in black sand, and there were tiers of crowded seats set all around it. In the very centre of the seats was the royal box, with a canopy over it. Two large iron thrones were set up in there, one for the Queen, one for the General. Neither was there yet.

It was very noisy and smelly, and lit by a weird red glow. Thomas's legs suddenly felt weak, but there was no turning back – the soldiers pushed him in. They brought him to a seat just below the royal box, near a deafening squad of uniformed drummers. Everyone stared at Thomas, who took no notice. He was too busy staring at what was in the centre of the arena.

There were many cages stacked up on each other on the sandy floor. In each cage was a creature. He could only clearly see a few of them: a two-headed dwarf, a lion-headed thing with a snake's body, a small, desperate-eyed dragon. They were clearly terrified, their roaring and growling and hissing and screaming mingling with the yells of the crowd and the drumming. And no wonder they were scared, for just a little distance from them was a large, sinister-looking crack in the floor of the stadium, whose edges glowed bright, bright red, so bright that it hurt your eyes if you looked at it for too long.

Deepfire! thought Thomas, clutching the arms of his chair. At that moment, a trumpet blast sounded shrilly over the rest of the noise. Everyone in the arena fell on their knees. Everyone, that is, except for Thomas, who had simply stood up. General Legion Morningstar

and Queen Lilith swept into the arena, Fustian Jargon and Salmagundo Firewalker at their sides, and a colourful crowd of courtiers behind them.

The Queen was as beautiful and cruel-looking as her portrait. She was almost as tall as her son, and together they made a striking pair, he in his red and black armour, she in a sheath of what looked like pure gold. They held Thomas's gaze, blankly, and he found himself bowing without meaning to. Then they nodded, and went to their seats. With a great rustle, the crowd rose from their knees, and Thomas sat down, too. There was another trumpet blast, a great loud burst on the drums. A tall, handsome black-haired man in long dark robes and with black leathery wings sprouting from his shoulders, came striding into the arena. He was carrying a strangely-shaped staff that glowed like fire. He held up a hand for quiet.

'It is my duty and my pleasure, as my Lord

and Lady's Master of Ceremonies, to open the Deepfire Festival!' he said, in a huge, booming voice. 'May our Lord and our Lady live for ever!'

He stepped to one side and clicked his fingers. Instantly, two enormous, shambling trolls appeared. They went straight to the cages, opened four, and took out the creatures. Holding them up in huge, meaty paws, they displayed the struggling things to the crowd: the two-headed dwarf, the small dragon, a thing that looked rather like a relative of Guesty's, and a limp toad-headed thing that appeared as if it were already dead. The Master of Ceremonies shouted, 'These creatures have used up their usefulness, and must go to Deepfire! Open, o eternal flame!' So saying, he tapped with his staff on the sand.

With a deafening, rending sound, the crack opened wider. Wider, wider still; molten red lava pouring from it, so much that it seemed it must soon cover the whole floor. But just as it got near the trolls' feet (and they hadn't even moved, their stupid faces showing no fear at all), the Master of Ceremonies tapped with the staff again, and the lava stopped. Then, quite suddenly, the trolls opened their paws, and dropped the yelling, struggling creatures they were holding straight on to the lava. It immediately wrapped itself around them, just like a spider spinning its victims in silk, and rushed with them to the lip of the crack. In they went, and disappeared, in less time than it takes to think it.

The crowd erupted into wild cheers and stomps and claps. Overcome with horror, Thomas turned to the Queen and the General. They were smiling. Smiling! His stomach turned over at the sight. No, there was no mercy to be had in this place.

He felt for the salamander talisman. Just as he did so, something light and extremely strong landed on top of him, dragging him backwards, and he heard a familiar voice whispering, 'Be quiet. The spell-net will last for a few minutes. Should be enough. It makes you invisible, if you keep your mouth tight shut.'

Hinkypunk! thought Thomas. He couldn't see the trickster, though he could hear him. He could make out nothing but muffled, moving shapes. It was like being wrapped up in cotton wool. 'We'll get you out soon enough, my dear,' said another voice; and Thomas's heart leaped as he recognised Angelica's tones. Patch must have made it through, he thought, wildly relieved. Thank goodness, thank goodness, Patch must have made it through!

But he was thanking goodness too early. For at that moment, a horribly familiar, light, toneless voice resounded in his ear. 'Not so fast, Middler! The Rymer is *ours*!'

'What do you mean, *yours*?' Angelica Eyebright's voice was scornful. 'How can he be yours? No Rymer has ever belonged to Uncouther lands. You know that.'

'No Rymer has ever stayed in our lands *before*!'

said the General. 'But this one has now. He has
been a guest with us. He has eaten our food,
drunk our drink. He wears our salamander
talisman.'

'You forced them on him!'

The General's voice was full of triumph. 'No.
He took everything of his own free will.'

Silence. In his spell-net, Thomas's heart
sank. All at once, things became quite clear to
him. He'd been tricked! None of the
Uncouthers had spoken the truth to him. They
were not going to cast him into Deepfire –
they just wanted him to stay here for ever, and
by accepting their food, drink and talisman,
that's just what would happen. He should have
refused everything in this place. But how could
he have known?

'He's a young Rymer,' said Angelica. For the
first time ever her voice was uncertain. 'He
doesn't know a lot of things yet about our
world. It isn't fair. You know that, General. You
know the rules of our world.'

'He does indeed. But what do they matter to him?' A new voice: soft, silky, well-bred. The voice of Mr Tamblin!

'Mr Tamblin,' said Angelica Eyebright, sharply, 'whose side are you on?'

'Mine, dear Miss Eyebright, of course,' rejoined Mr Tamblin. 'Mine, and Aspire's. Which comes to the same thing.'

As he spoke, suddenly there came a loud 'pop!' and the spell-net dissolved. Thomas jumped up, and saw Angelica, Hinkypunk, Mr Tamblin, and a little round woman, holding a silver flute, standing around him on the black sand. Just behind them were the Queen, the General, and Fustian.

'Oh, damn,' said Hinkypunk. No one else said anything; but the General and the Queen smiled, nastily.

'I'm not staying here,' said Thomas, into the silence. He tried to throw the salamander talisman away from him, but it stuck to his fingers. 'You tricked and betrayed me into doing what you wanted. You can't make me stay!'

'Oh, but we can,' said the Queen, speaking for the first time. Her voice was as ice-cold as her looks.

'*Oh, but she can,*' echoed Mr Tamblin. Everyone glared at him. Ignoring this, he went on. 'She can, indeed, but there's just one small thing. I'm sure the great Queen and the General will not have overlooked it, of course.'

Hinkypunk nodded. There was a thin smile dawning on his face.

'You will have *invited* him into your country, of course?' said Mr Tamblin, softly. 'Invited him, and called him by his *name* as you did so? Of course, you won't have neglected that.'

The General stirred. Sharply, he said, 'You don't have to be invited into Nightmare. You can be pulled in. And, I believe, nor do you need a name; it's enough to be an Obbo.'

'If you're an ordinary Obbo, yes,' said Mr Tamblin, shaking his head. 'But a Rymer?'

'That's an old idea,' said the General, uncertainly. 'We've gone past it.' He turned to Fustian Jargon hovering at his back. 'Is that not so?'

Fustian Jargon shuffled his feet. 'Well, sir, Lord General, that is—'

'Don't be a fool,' snapped the Queen. 'A Rymer is quite different from other humans. What sort of adviser are you, if you don't know that?'

She turned to Thomas. 'Were you invited? Did my son call you by name?'

'Course not,' said Thomas, indignantly. 'He doesn't know my name. I didn't tell him. And no one invited me. I fell in through a hole in Monsieur Reynard's shop,' he went on, looking pointedly at Mr Tamblin, who winced elegantly.

'It's hard to control an artist, they do what they want, don't you know,' Mr Tamblin murmured. 'But I'll tell him he has to shut that illusion down, pronto.'

The Queen's eyes were like narrow blue shards of ice as she rounded furiously on her son. 'You fool! You lied to me! You said you'd invited him! Why?'

'Because, Mother,' said the General, angrily, 'because you would not have agreed to trick him into staying if I had told you the truth. You are so set in your ways. I would have got around those problems. He would have told us his name, in time!'

Queen Lilith snarled, 'It had to be straight away for it to really work! Those old ways of ours that you mock, my son, have served us well. We are the undisputed masters of nightmare and terror. What would you put against that? Your crackpot theories? What's wrong with you?'

'You never want to try anything new,' shouted the General.

How odd, thought Thomas, he no longer looks quite so tall, or quite so scary. Has he shrunk, inside his armour? Lilith Morningstar's mouth was set in a thin line. 'You're a rash fool. Crown Prince you may be, but Crown Prince you may well remain for ever! From now on, you will have to bring all decisions to me first. We have a treaty with the Middlers, the Ariels, the Montaynards and the Seafolk. I don't like this treaty any more than you do. But I don't like these dangerous games of yours either. They could destroy us. One war was quite enough. Release the Rymer at once,' she said, coldly.

Turning on her heel, she swept out of the arena, a flock of anxious courtiers at her heels, including Salmagundo Firewalker. Just as they went out, the Deepfire diver turned and looked at Thomas. Thomas was never quite sure afterwards if he'd imagined it, but he thought he saw the Deepfire diver wink at him, just before he disappeared with the others. At the same moment, Thomas felt an unpleasant wriggle in his hands; and the salamander talisman slid out, landing on the floor at his feet and slithering like a snake towards the Deepfire crack, where it disappeared!

'I'm so sorry, dear General,' said Mr Tamblin, lightly, 'but I think this is where we say farewell to all you lovely people and take Thomas back home.'

The General spun round on him. 'You little rats,' he yelled, 'you won't get away with this! I'll catch you, I'll boil you alive, I'll roast you in Deepfire, I'll . . .'

Yes, most definitely the General is smaller, Thomas thought. And his eyes, that had been so dark and frightening in their blankness, were full of real feeling. And that feeling was fury. Helpless fury. His face was purpling, his fists were clenched, he looked like he wanted to scream and roll on the ground and drum his heels. It made him look almost . . . almost funny!

Suddenly, Thomas could not stop the giggle that began in his chest and travelled up into his throat from erupting out of his mouth. He laughed and laughed in the General's face, and the General's face got more and more purple. He loomed threateningly over Thomas, and there's no telling what might have happened if at that moment Hinkypunk hadn't stepped in, briskly. In his hand, he held something small and yellow and wriggling.

'Your Ironheartedness,' he purred, 'these fools may have come to insult you, but I am partly of the blood of Nightmare, and I have come to offer you a gift.'

'A gift?' said the General, pausing. 'What gift?'

'The best gift for one so gifted as yourself,' said Hinkypunk smoothly, ignoring the others' glares. 'I call it a yallery.' He winked rapidly at Thomas, as if to warn him to be quiet, and held the wriggling, spitting, yellow creature out to the General. 'This creature's function is to be an echo, General. It will amplify your every word, like a megaphone. It will spread your ideas throughout Nightmare. It might one day persuade others to follow your new, modern ways, and not the . . . er . . . old ones.'

The General glared suspiciously at him. He snatched up the yallery. 'I am the greatest one who ever lived,' he said. Instantly, the yallery boomed, in a voice that echoed round and round the arena, 'I am the greatest one who ever lived.'

'I will ride up from Nightmare into the world above,' went on the General, with a wicked look at the Middlers. The yallery repeated this, very loudly.

'Your Gorgeousness,' whispered Fustian Jargon, anxiously, 'this may be a deceitful trick. This creature may not be best suited to—'

'Shut up, Fustian,' said the General, loudly, stroking the thick spiky skin of the yallery. 'You don't seem to truly understand the greatness of my person, as this creature does.'

'Shut up, Fustian,' said the yallery, loudly. 'You don't seem to truly understand the greatness of my person, as this creature does.'

The look Fustian gave the yallery then would have frizzled up a much bigger creature.

But the ugly little thing was unconcerned, settling in happily on the General's shoulder.

The General laughed.

'Ah, so, Fustian Jargon, you foolish, useless so-called adviser, you're jealous, now?' he hissed, and the yallery faithfully repeated his words. By now, all the other Uncouthers in the stadium were laughing and laughing at Fustian's embarrassment and dismay. No one paid any attention at all as Thomas and his friends slipped quietly out of the arena, and into the laneways of Pandemonium.

'Hinkypunk,' said Mr Tamblin, 'that was a clever idea. Set them against one another, that's the ticket.'

'I'm so pleased you think so, Mr Tamblin,' said Hinkypunk, sarcastically. 'That does make me feel warm inside.'

'Oh, good, then,' said Mr Tamblin,

nonchalantly. 'As for me, I'm off. I've had quite enough of the smells of this place. Pooh! You'd think the Uncouthers might clean up once in a while!'

And with these words, he clicked a hand in the air, and vanished. Angelica stood there an instant, shaking her head. 'You'll never change those ones,' she muttered, crossly, then turned to Thomas. 'We thought you weren't ready to fight them. But Thomas, you showed you were able to resist the power of Nightmare on your own! You are *truly* a Rymer.'

'I thought of Mum,' said Thomas, quietly. 'I saw her in my head, you know. I heard the music she used to play. It made me stronger.'

'Ah! And you knew also to hide your name from them.'

'I didn't *know*,' said Thomas, honestly. 'I thought maybe – in stories sometimes they say a name gives power. I thought they might have power over me if I told them. But I wasn't sure. Anyway, I *didn't* know not to take anything from them.' He looked around him, and shivered. 'I could have been stuck here for ever . . .'

'Nonsense!' said Angelica Eyebright, a little too heartily. 'We would have found a way of getting you out. And you've done a great thing – the Queen will be keeping an eagle eye on her son from now on. As will we. I doubt he'll give up his plans altogether. But for the moment, we can breathe easy again. Now then, my dear, take my hand, and Hinkypunk's. Right, Calliope Nightingale, we're ready,' she said, nodding to the little woman. 'Play us the song of the Rymer to take us back through the passages into our own land.'

'This was written by your mother, Thomas,' said Calliope Nightingale, smiling, 'but I've added a new verse – the verse of our own new Rymer, Thomas Trew, who is the first ever to pass unscathed through the land of the Uncouthers.'

She put the flute to her mouth and began to play. It was a beautiful, haunting tune. As she played, Thomas could see pictures: other Rymers, some dressed in modern clothes, some in old-fashioned ones, and everywhere around them, the sharp little faces, the watchers of the Hidden World. He felt himself carried up on the current of his mother's melody, wafted back up through the dark passages of Pandemonium, through the rock of the underground, and back into the soft green countryside of the Middlers. He could see all those people who had been like him, their faces floating before him. And then, suddenly, there was his mother, the flute to her lips, her face turned towards him, glowing with love and tenderness. He did not know he had tears in his eyes, only that he had a glow as warm as sunshine in his heart.

And then he was back on Owlchurch green. His father was the first to reach him. He hugged Thomas tightly. All around was a crowd of smiling, cheering villagers. Then suddenly there was a shout, and Pinch and Patch dashed through the crowd towards him. 'Thomas! Thomas! You're safe!'

'Yes,' said Thomas. He looked at Patch. 'I owe you lots, Patch. I'd never have got out of there!'

'Don't be silly,' said Patch, flushing, but looking very pleased. 'You did most of it on your own. Anyway, what are friends for?'

Pinch hopped up and down impatiently, a bit jealous. 'Hey, are we going to stand about all day here? They're going to start making speeches in a moment, if we're not careful. And then we'll be stuck here for ages!'

'OK. Race you to the river,' laughed Thomas, and he was off, running as hard as he could, the Gull twins panting at his heels.

There would be time enough later to talk and think about all that had happened. But not right now. It was a sunny morning in

Owlchurch, the Riddle sparkled like liquid diamonds, and his friends were with him.

The darkness and fear of the Land of Nightmare slipped from him as he ran, his feet making hardly any sound in the soft long grass.

Thomas Trew and the Horns of Pan

Sophie Masson

Thomas loves living in the Hidden World. His friends, the twins Pinch and Patch, are even teaching him magic, like how to make himself invisible.

Then a beautiful stranger comes to Owlchurch. She holds the Horns of Pan, the Hidden World's highest award for magic.

Everyone is very excited – except Thomas and the twins. Something very odd is going on, and they're determined to find out . . .